WEAVERS OF THE CRYSTAL DOMES

Book One of KUDZU WORLDS

SUZANNE STRANGE

iUniverse, Inc.
Bloomington

Weavers of the Crystal Domes
Book One of Kudzu Worlds

iUniverse books may be ordered through booksellers or by contacting:

iUniverse
1663 Liberty Drive
Bloomington, IN 47403
www.iuniverse.com
1-800-Authors (1-800-288-4677)

ISBN: 978-1-4620-1450-7 (sc)
ISBN: 978-1-4620-1451-4 (e)
ISBN: 978-1-4620-1452-1 (dj)

Printed in the United States of America

iUniverse rev. date: 02/25/2012

DEDICATED TO TRADER BILL

꧁ ꧂ ꧁ ꧂ ꧁ ꧂ ꧁ ꧂ ꧁ ꧂ ꧁

acknowledgements

I wish to thank friends and family members who dared me to write the story I had been talking about for twenty years, and graciously helped me to do so with their encouragement, suggestions, and frank criticism. Without their help, this book would never have been written.

Google and Wikipedia, the modern writer's friends, were invaluable research aids, and even more so were two fascinating books by Southern authors: "Despicable Species" by Janet Lembke and "Kudzu in America" by Juanitta Baldwin.

Contents

PART ONE:

how kudzu saved our world

chapτer one:
luna

"As if she had found wings, light as the wind"
from "The Wakers" by John Freeman

Beneath a sparkling crystal dome sprawled Queen City Middle School, a roofless brick building three stories high where Ruth Weller had spent thirty years teaching English to restless seventh and eighth graders. On the first day of the 2115-2116 school year, she stood beside her pod and greeted students as they filed into her classroom and found their seats. The teardrop-shaped pod, with built-in seat, desk, computer, and storage compartments, was parked near the classroom's left front corner, allowing students a clear view of the multi-screen monitor that filled the front wall.

On stackable plastic chairs, students sat in groups of four at long narrow tables embedded with touch-screen keyboards. In the Wi-Fied classroom, students used the keyboards to download information from the monitor, process it with computers built into their eyeware,[1] and store it in their personal data chips.[2]

On that day, Ms. Weller presented a writing assignment to

---

1 Eyewear with a microcomputer built into its frame and temples.
2 Computer chip implanted between a student's skin and cranium, usually behind the right ear.

all her eighth grade classes. At the beginning of every period she explained the assignment carefully:

"During the next four weeks each of you will write an essay in the form of an autobiography at least five hundred words long. This will be done in addition to your other assignments. During that time we shall be reviewing grammar, sentence structure, and punctuation. We shall also read and analyze excerpts from biographies and autobiographies of famous people."

In every class, someone asked, "Ms. Weller, what's an autobiography?"

"It's the story of your life," was her inevitable response. "Look it up. On the board behind me you'll see AUTOBIOGRAPHY neatly printed so you can find it in your dictionaries. I want each of you to write about important events in your life, what you did, what you learned, and how you feel. Tell what you plan to be doing twenty years from now. Think about what you want to say. Writing an autobiography will help you understand yourself and clarify your goals in life."

In every class, the question was asked, "Is it okay if I write about somebody else instead?"

Her response was always, "No, it is not 'okay.' All of you have dictionaries in your data chips. Please look up the definition of 'autobiography.' No more questions. Anyone who has written at least two hundred words may bring the unfinished work to me for comment. I'll be glad to look it over and make suggestions if you need help."

After the last student in the last class had left, Ruth Weller settled into her pod. She opened a small drawer, took out a bag of candy, and poured several Hershey's Kisses onto her desk. "Hello there," she whispered to the chocolates. "I've been thinking about you all day."

Four weeks later, Ms. Weller stood before the first period class, most of her students watching her attentively through the lenses of their school-issued eyeware, hoping to not be asked to read, recite, or venture an opinion on anything. One girl was the exception, her eyeware resting on the table before her as she gazed absently at something – most likely nothing – beyond the teacher's left shoulder.

"Before we download your autobiographies," said Ms. Weller, "I'd like one of you to read yours to the class. Do I have a volunteer?"

No hands were raised. "Fine," she thought. "We'll start with the Moon child." She looked directly at the daydreamer, and in a firm clear voice announced, "Miss Reyes, let's hear what you have to say."

"It never fails," thought Luna. "Whenever she doesn't know who else to call on, my name pops right out of her mouth." Luna stood up, put on her eyeware, and walked to the front of the classroom. The microcomputer's right temple pressed against her skin over an implanted data chip, the right lens was a monitor, transparent when not in use, and the left temple held a small earbud. Luna touched the right temple to activate the monitor, and began reading aloud as her essay scrolled before her eye:

"My name is Luna Reyes. I was born September 11, 2101 in a town called Mega City, on the far side of the Moon, and lived there until I was five years old. Everybody worked for Mega Mining, and they had come from nearly every country on Earth. They all wanted to celebrate the same holidays they had back home, so there seemed to be a parade somewhere in Mega City nearly every week. Santa Claus paid us a visit every Christmas Eve before making his rounds on Earth.

"I spent most of my time playing with friends in the Children's Center. The Center had a big room with lots of toys and a playground with swings, slides, and plenty of space to play games. We learned to sing, count to ten, and speak a few phrases in several languages. I can still remember most of the things they taught us.

"On weekends, I went exploring with my parents, holding

their hands as I walked between them. They used to lift me off the ground and swing me back and forth while they were walking. I loved for them to do that. We visited the greenhouses every week. Mama taught me the names of all the plants and insects we saw there. 'Greenhouses are the Moon's Garden of Eden. A greenhouse is a holy place,' my mother used to say. I was always on my best behavior there. Sometimes my parents took me outside the complex, away from habitat gravity, so I could bounce around in my spacesuit. That was my very favorite thing to do.

"When I moved to North Carolina and saw kudzu for the first time, I didn't know what to think. The only outside world I had ever seen before was the surface of the Moon, and nothing grows there.

"I had never seen anything growing outside a greenhouse before. I thought the kudzu was creepy-looking, and I was afraid it would reach out and grab me.

"Now I am used to the kudzu and the rain and I like living here. I have learned about music from my grandfather and weaving from my grandmother. My parents and grandparents even taught me to use an agbelt [3] when I was only five years old. I outgrew the belt several years ago, but didn't get another because I am so busy with other things. When I need a belt for a school project my teacher gets me one from the supply room.

"I like to do things with my friends. We take dancing and karate lessons together. Last year, my friend Ellie and I made up a funny dance routine that combined ballet and karate moves. Susie and Abby performed with us and we won third place in the seventh grade talent contest.

"I'm not sure what I want to do when I grow up, probably something to do with science or health. Maybe I'll be a safety inspector for Mega Corporation and live on the Moon like my parents did."

"Very nice, Miss Reyes," said her teacher.

3　Antigravity belt

"Thank you, Ms. Weller," Luna replied. She turned off her eyeware and returned to her seat.

Charles Reyes and Jenna Becker worked for the Moon Exploration Division of Mega Mining Corporation. Charles, a young structural engineer with a sturdy build and a serious demeanor, was a building inspector. One afternoon in 2099, he walked unannounced into the greenhouse where Jenna was working, showed her his company ID, and told her he was there for a safety inspection.

"I'm a safety inspector too," said Jenna. "I worked a couple of years in a testing lab for the FDA,[4] then took this job because I like to travel. What about you?"

"I started with Mega right out of college," replied Charles. "I wanted to see the world, and this seemed like a good way to do it. Or maybe not. So far I haven't seen much except the Moon."

Their conversation continued through that night's dinner and many more meals as mutual attraction deepened into love. Later that year they married and moved into a small apartment in the downtown area of EGH, the earth gravity habitat. In 2101, shortly after the birth of their daughter Luna, they rented a larger apartment in the EGH neighborhood known as "the burb."

Luna was curious and energetic, always on the move. When she was three years old, her parents rented a small pink spacesuit and started taking her outside the habitat to play. She loved to jump again and again, bending her knees as she landed, then springing up and forward with all her strength, keeping her legs straight behind her as she pretended to be a grasshopper like those she saw in the greenhouses.

One Sunday evening, after an afternoon of Moon-hopping, Luna had a question for her father. "Daddy, can you get me a green suit?" she asked him.

"What's wrong with the one you have?" he wanted to know.

"I see lots of insects in the greenhouses," Luna said, "but I've

4   US Food and Drug Administration

never seen a pink grasshopper. Can't you get me a green suit so I'll look more grasshopperish?"

"Sweetheart," her father told her, "What you really look like is a kite trying to get off the ground!" And he was right about that, as Luna's spacesuit was always connected to his by a long pink tether.

"Daddy, what's a kite?" she asked.

Charles tried to explain about using wind to fly kites, but Luna couldn't understand what a kite was, or wind either. She had never felt wind on the Moon.

That night, after Luna was asleep, Jenna told her husband to stop teasing the child and let her pretend to be whatever she wanted to be. "What she really wants to be," said Charles, "Is free of the tether that keeps her from disappearing over the nearest hill." Jenna had to agree with him about that.

The next day, Jenna called Spacesuit Rentals to see if they had children's suits in any colors other than pink and yellow. "Are they available in green?" she asked.

"No," said the receptionist, "Pink and yellow are easiest to see from a distance, except for white or orange, which are reserved for adults. We don't carry them in green. We usually assign pink suits to girls and yellow suits to boys, but there's no reason why a boy can't wear pink or a girl can't wear yellow. Would you like to exchange your daughter's suit for a yellow one?"

"I'll let you know," said Jenna. "Thank you for the information."

That night Jenna told her daughter that, although rare, there were such things as pink grasshoppers, but green spacesuits in a child's size did not seem to exist.

"Some grasshoppers are yellow," she said. "I've seen a couple of them. You decide what to do. You can be the first pink grasshopper on the Moon, or swap your pink suit for a yellow one and be a yellow grasshopper instead." Luna decided to stick with pink, and the issue was settled.

Much later, when a teen-age Luna told this story to her

friends, she admitted that even though she had wanted to look like a grasshopper in a green spacesuit, she had wanted even more not to look like a boy in a yellow one!

Shortly after Luna's fifth birthday, her parents were transferred to Mega Mining North America, headquartered in western North Carolina. Coming from the dust-gray Moon to the kudzu-green Earth was an eye-opener for the little girl, who remained glued to her window during the entire hovercraft trip from the Virginia spaceport.

It was late afternoon when they approached the Charlotte airport, the sky's usual grayness yielding to a brilliant sunset. As their craft, circling to land, turned away from the setting sun, Luna saw a spectacular blaze of red, orange and yellow bursting from the kudzu below. She tugged at her mother's sleeve. "Look!" she cried. "Is that a fire?" She knew about fire, but had never seen one.

Jenna looked out the window. "No, Sweetheart," she said. "That's not fire. Charlotte's crystal domes are reflecting the sunset. We're home at last."

Soon Luna and her parents were living beneath a crystal dome, sharing an apartment with Philip and May Becker, Luna's Poppy and Grammy.

In his role of building inspector, Charles regularly visited many of Mega Mining's US operations. Jenna traveled with him, inspecting greenhouses and kitchens at every site. They were often away for weeks at a time, leaving Luna with her grandparents in a world very different from the unchanging Moon.

Luna had been brought to a world where violent storms appeared without warning and daytime skies suddenly darkened as gusting winds sent torrents of rain swirling about her new home. The little girl trembled with fear when thunder boomed incessantly and lightning streaked the sodden skies above the crystal dome.

From a circle of lightning rods atop the dome, insulated wires snaked downward through a crystal forest into huge underground storage batteries. When lightning struck the metal rods, distant booms were replaced by deafening thunderclaps and flashes of unbearable brightness pierced the dome. As the storm's furious energy raced harmlessly to the ground, the crystals resonated like the strings of a giant harp, enveloping Luna's body in waves of sound.

"Come here, Little One," Grammy would say, wrapping her arms around the frightened child. "That's just the music of the dome. The storm will soon be over and everything will be all right." Eventually Luna realized that Grammy was right. Safe within her singing dome, she would no longer be afraid.

Earth weather aside, life with Luna's grandparents could be great fun.

Poppy explained the musical scale and taught her to play simple tunes on a small keyboard. He taught her the words to a lot of old-fashioned songs, too. Her favorite, "I Want To Hold Your Hand," reminded her of walking through Mega City with her parents. She and Poppy often sang it together when he walked her to and from school.

Grammy was an accomplished basketmaker, and often had lengths of kudzu strung up to season throughout their home. She taught Luna to make small toys and baskets from kudzu vines. The little girl practiced for hours, making tiny furniture for her dolls and a dome for them to live in. Grammy even helped her make a small stool, tightly woven and sturdy enough to sit on.

One day Poppy walked through the front door and looked around at the latest batch of vines hanging everywhere. "I feel like I'm living underground," he said, "with roots reaching down to grab hold of me." Luna giggled at that idea, but Grammy didn't think it was the least bit funny.

Although Moon residents live by Earth's clock and calendar, an actual Moon day lasts about four Earth weeks, with two weeks of bright daylight and two weeks of total darkness. When Luna finally adjusted to Earth's rapid cycles of light and dark, she realized happily that Earth was always dark when it was time to sleep and light when it was time to play.

She discovered other differences the first time Mama and Daddy took her for a walk outside the dome. She was pleased that she didn't need a bulky spacesuit, just goggles attached to a small oxygen mask. Best of all, there was no tether. She would be unrestrained, able to move about freely.

Eagerly Luna stepped outside, holding her parents' hands as they walked together along the wide strip of bare ground around the dome. "This is great," she thought. But then she discovered something strange. When they released her hands, she couldn't jump high at all, no matter how hard she tried. She could hop a tiny bit, but she wasn't able to leap like a grasshopper as she had done before.

Shocked and disappointed, Luna began to cry, tears spilling from her hazel eyes and pooling in her goggles. Alarmed, Charles picked up the sobbing child and carried her back into the crystal dome, her wavy brown hair flowing over his arm while Jenna walked alongside trying to comfort her.

That night, the four adults took turns holding Luna on their laps as they attempted to explain Earth's gravity. They all tried to assure her that gravity was a good thing even if it did ruin her favorite game, but she kept thinking the Moon was more fun and she intended to live there again someday.

The next morning, Charles called the office of Mega Mining's training director and made an appointment to see Director John Williams. That afternoon he and Poppy traveled by zipcar through a subterranean tunnel connecting the Charlotte complex with Mega Mining's administration dome. Once there, the men showed their credentials to the security guards and were ushered into the training director's spacious office.

"It's good to see you again, my friend," said John, shaking hands with Charles. "And it's good to meet you, Mr. Becker," he said, turning to Poppy. "Now both of you sit down and tell me about this pressing personal matter you need my help with."

Luna's father explained the situation, and soon the three men were smiling broadly.

"Bless her heart," said John. "We'll have to do something for your daughter right away. You and Jenna are two of Mega's most valuable employees, and we want your family to be as happy here as you were on the Moon." He stood up. "Let's adjourn to the training dome and continue our conversation there."

Lining the dome's curved wall were tools, parts of disassembled structures, and mysterious pieces of equipment ready for use in training exercises. Scattered throughout the dome were groups of engineers and technicians hovering over their work. One group was assembling a spidery-looking object that Charles guessed was a microwave tower of the type used on the Moon.

After their tour of the training dome, the men parted with smiles and handshakes all around. Charles and Philip caught the next zipcar to the Charlotte complex, where they hurried home, arriving in time for Charles to have a few minutes of conversation with his wife and mother-in-law before supper. While the others were talking, Poppy and Luna were in another room playing the keyboard and singing. Then they all walked together to the dining hall.

After the family had finished their meal and returned home, Luna played cards with her Mama and Daddy until bedtime, while Grammy worked on a basket and Poppy read a Mega Mining training manual.

Two weeks later, a package addressed to Luna Reyes was delivered to their apartment. Charles opened it and told his daughter to look inside. Luna peered into the box, but wasn't sure what she was seeing. "Take your present out and show it to us," her father told her.

He held the box while Jenna helped their daughter lift out a very small agbelt. "Consider this an early birthday present," Jenna said. "Daddy and I have to leave in a couple of weeks. We'll miss your birthday and won't be home again until Thanksgiving. This belt will help you jump like a grasshopper right here on Earth.

You can learn to fly like a butterfly and even turn somersaults if you want to."

Luna shrieked with joy. "This is the best thing that ever happened to me!" She ran around the room hugging everybody, then plopped herself down on the couch, where she sat until bedtime with her birthday present on her lap.

The next day, tethered first between Daddy and Poppy and then between Mama and Grammy, Luna had her first agbelt lessons in Mega Mining's huge training dome. It was one of the happiest days of her life, and would always be her fondest childhood memory.

chapter two:
kudzu

"The vine that ate the South"

Southern epithet – Source Unknown

Kudzu was introduced to America in 1876 at the Centennial Exposition in Philadelphia. Through the early 1900s, it was widely used in the South to control erosion and enrich the soil.

By 1976, kudzu was smothering the Southeast, growing twelve inches a day over trees, fences and anything else that couldn't move. It was difficult to control and almost impossible to kill. Cut to the ground, dug up by the roots, burned, poisoned, and paved over, the sturdy vines always returned, slipping through cracks in concrete, bursting through asphalt, thriving where nothing else could live. Patches of kudzu were found in forty-eight states and southern Canada. Invasive and unwelcome, kudzu showed up everywhere, making few friends and many enemies.

Surprisingly, during the twenty-first century, kudzu saved our world. This is how it happened:

In 2034 an 8.1 earthquake unzipped the entire San Andreas fault, causing part of Southern California to crumble into the Pacific Ocean. National Guard units from the Carolinas joined units from all over the nation to help with rescue and clean-up operations in California. South Carolina's first public shelters were dug into and around Paris Mountain, a few miles north of Greenville.

In 2036 the great caldera of Yellowstone exploded, covering the park with lava, showering neighboring states with volcanic ash and causing rapid deterioration in air quality worldwide. Again National Guard units from around the county rushed to help. In South Carolina, excavation had begun into the heart of Piney Mountain, a sandy hill at Paris Mountain's southern end, gouging out space to store medical goods, food, tools, cots, blankets, clothing, fuel cells, air purifiers, and other supplies. Greenhouses were built in caves dug around the mountain's base. A few miles away, a small nuclear fusion power plant was under construction in an old quarry.

In 2037, when Hurricane Jethro hit the South Carolina Coast, sending a storm surge sixty miles inland, thousands of evacuees escaped to the upstate and into Paris Mountain's emergency shelters. The shelters were needed again a few weeks later when people fled before Hurricane Pete as it bore down on the central part of the state, flattening the Columbia area. Vegetables grown in underground greenhouses fed both groups of refugees. Later, a factory was built to process kudzu roots into a protein-rich powder, and a small cannery was added.

In 2038 a series of earthquakes in Missouri changed the course of the Mississippi River, causing unprecedented flooding in several states that left millions homeless. Kudzu powder and canned vegetables were sent to the survivors.

In 2039, work was finished on another group of underground shelters, with the help of civic-minded volunteers and ankle-braceleted community service workers. Connected by subterranean passageways, the new bunkers encircled the mountain fortress, doubling shelter capacity. More greenhouses were added and the cannery enlarged. Across the nation, other communities were taking similar actions.

Although the US and other industrialized nations had finally embraced "green technology," most developing countries had continued to follow the smokestack example of the nineteenth and twentieth centuries. Air quality worldwide had deteriorated so badly by late 2039 that masks or small oxygen concentrators were commonly worn outdoors. In the United States, entertainment and sporting events were no longer held in the open air, and most plant life struggled to survive. Produce growers invested heavily in greenhouses. Kudzu alone remained green and healthy, covering abandoned farms and dying forests with its lush green blanket.

On New Year's Day, 2040, a 5.9 earthquake felt as far north as Connecticut destroyed the northern South Carolina city of Rock Hill, taking several lives. The quake and its aftershocks caused considerable damage in North Carolina as well, leaving highways in the Charlotte area strewn with abandoned vehicles.

In February, a series of tremors shook South Carolina's lowcountry. Charleston's buildings, reinforced over the years to survive hurricanes and storm surges, suffered little damage. Things were much worse in small towns and rural areas, but no lives were lost. Most South Carolinians felt that the worst was over.

They were wrong. More trouble was on the way. Running parallel to the North Carolina border in three western South Carolina counties, the Brevard fault had slipped occasionally over the years, unnoticed by nearly everyone but seismologists. That year, on May 25, it burst apart in a quake registering 7.1 on the Richter scale, damaging a nuclear power plant in Oconee County and toppling buildings up to fifty miles away. Downtown Greenville lay in ruins. Across the upstate, water mains broke and gas lines ruptured, and fires broke out everywhere with no way to extinguish them as they swept across the countryside, fed by the brittle fuel of dying forests.

Even kudzu burned to the ground, reappearing during the next rainy season in the form of pale green tendrils peering bravely above the sodden ashes, tiny leaves unfolding along their sides as they reached upward. After the rains ended in November, a dry and unusually mild winter began. With no frost to trigger its annual winter dieback, kudzu spread luxuriantly across the ruined land.

Martial law, in effect nationwide since the Yellowstone eruption four years earlier, was now an accepted way of life, maintaining order in a nation besieged by forty years of global war and a string of natural disasters. Sending armed forces around the world while fending off terrorists at home, the federal government could no longer provide food and shelter for the nation's displaced civilians. Everything, no matter how difficult, must now be done locally.

Survivors of the earthquakes and fires took refuge in Greenville's shelters, filling them beyond capacity. After the fires died down, a tent city housing three thousand single men sprang up near Paris Mountain, lessening the chaos of shelter life for the people remaining in the bunkers. Order was eventually restored and several acres southwest of the mountain were cleared for new construction.

With borrowed equipment, money for building supplies lent by Canadian and Brazilian banks, and a plentiful supply of skilled and unskilled labor, construction of the first habitat dome began in January 2041. One year later, refugees began moving from the shelters into apartment buildings clustered beneath the huge steel-framed glass dome. Another dome was in the planning stages.

In the poisoned atmosphere of the outside world, kudzu alone continued to flourish, flaunting large clusters of fragrant purple blossoms as it twined over and into every ruin, turning the Carolinas into an impenetrable jungle. There were many uses for the ubiquitous vines. Wild kudzu became furniture, containers, paper, and clothing. Shredded stems purified contaminated streams and rivers. Food-grade kudzu grown in huge greenhouses provided leaves to cook or use in salads, blossoms to make preserves, wine, and flavorings, and roots to process into a nutritious food additive.

Thousands of domed communities sprang up across the nation, steel and glass structures with air filtering systems. Newer domes built using structural carbon, lighter and stronger than steel, and spinel, a transparent ceramic stronger than glass, were more durable but equally expensive. A new approach was needed.

On a September day in 2047, two department heads and longtime friends approached each other in a Clemson faculty lounge. "How's it going with that "Architectural Uses Of Kudzu" course you started last year?" Gene Miller asked his colleague.

"Not bad," replied Dave Kraft, the elder of the two. He eased himself into an armchair and loosened his tie. "Students harvested vines at the beginning of last semester and hung them up to season, then spent the rest of the term designing structures. When the fall term starts tomorrow, I've got to teach them how to weave the stuff. I've been practicing all summer and now the arthritis in my hands is dealing me a fit."

"How can you teach them to weave with your hands like that?" asked Gene.

"Videos," said Dave. "They'll learn the same way I did, and I'll make them practice until they get it right." He motioned for his friend to sit in a nearby chair. "How are things with you?"

"Pretty good," said Gene, still standing. "I've been working with some grad students on a crystal-growing project. We're almost ready for field trials. Maybe your students can help us with something I want to try."

"So what do you have in mind?" asked Dave.

"Save that chair for me while I go and get us some coffee. I can't wait to tell you all about it!"

Gene left and David settled back, wondering what his friend was up to. David had heard rumors about something going on in the Materials Center. "This should be an interesting year," he thought. "If Gene's project is what I think it is, it could be a great year for all of us."

Gene reappeared with two cups of coffee and handed one to David. He sat down and began to explain his project. The two men talked excitedly for several hours.

The following week, in a large clearing near the Architectural Dome, Professor Kraft's students began building a group of upside-down kudzu baskets with open-weave designs he referred to as Buckminster[5] triangles. Perched airily on stilts about the clearing and surrounded by a swarm of busy students, the domes resembled a group of giant beehives.

In Clemson's Advanced Materials Center, Professor Miller and his team of Ph.D. candidates continued their experiments, developing a new growth-inducing compound to embed with tiny silicon dioxide "seeds." Chemical compounds known as crystallizers had been used to grow crystals in clean rooms since the mid-1900s, but Professor Miller and his group were pursuing an entirely new idea.

Professor Miller's graduate students were inspired by his vision of using Earth's most abundant plant and mineral resources to create a magnificent new form of architecture. Professor Kraft's students would share their dream. Silicon dioxide crystals would grow on woven kudzu, not in a lab under sterile conditions, but outdoors in Earth's heavily polluted atmosphere. It was the most exciting thing any of them had ever done.

When the domes were completed, the young architects and materials scientists coated every exposed surface with a thick layer of the seeded crystallizer. One month later, the crystallizer, now called Krystallizer, was applied again to the small crystals that now covered the woven kudzu.

Two weeks later, the rains began and exterior coating was halted for the duration. During the wet season, the crystals grew rapidly. Interior applications continued until crystals grew to fill all the triangular openings, sealing the dome. No more seeding was required. When the rains ended in May, the exterior was sprayed monthly with an unseeded solution called KrystalGrow. Exterior crystals melded at their bases to a thickness of several inches as new growth thrust jaggedly outward.

---

5   Buckminster Fuller was a noted twentieth century architect and dome designer.

Although Professor Kraft's students had returned to more traditional studies, they continued to assist with monthly applications of KrystalGrow until the rains returned in September. In January, the experiment was declared a success and the graduate students began writing their dissertations.

On May 25, 2049, a patent application for "A Method Of Inducing Rapid Large Scale Growth Of SiO^2 Crystals On A Kudzu Substrate In Standard Atmospheric Conditions" was filed by Professors Kraft and Miller and their teams, ushering in a new architectural period, the Crystal Domes Era.

On July 4, 2049, the jubilant students staged an impromptu light show in their field of domes. Since then, the clearing has been enlarged to hold first one, then two, then three crystal half-dome shells to hold stadium seating. Every year, rain or shine, large crowds gather to watch the Independence Day Light Show in the Field of Domes. It never fails to be a spectacular event.

chapter three:
michael

"Within your heart keep one still, secret spot
where dreams may go"

from "Hold Fast To Your Dreams"
by Louise Driscoll

n an October day in 2115, a Greenville boy read to his
eighth grade English class:

"My name is Michael Travis. My sister Megan and I
were born in Greenville, South Carolina on September 11, 2101,
the hundredth anniversary of the beginning of World War III.

"Our parents grew up here in the Greenville complex, attended
the Military Academy, and spent twenty years in service. They
came back here after they retired and got jobs with the County.

"I like to play Wii action games and I play real soccer and
basketball too. I like to go camping with my Dad. I like to
make things and fix things, and I like to read about olden times,
when people lived off the land and had to make everything they
needed.

"I try to do some pioneer things myself. I learned how to
make candles, but you aren't allowed to have any kind of fire in
the dome, so my Dad went outside with me one night and we lit
them there. I like to look at the pictures I took of them.

"I built a spinning wheel and tried to convince Megan to learn how to use it, but she didn't want to, so I'm trying to teach myself how to operate it. Megan says that if I spin wool or goat hair into yarn, she will knit me something out of it. Mom taught her how to knit a couple of years ago and she's pretty good at it. Mom just got a small loom and is learning how to use it. When she gets better at it, she's going to teach both of us how to weave.

"Sometimes when my Dad takes me camping we do a little hunting too. He taught me to use a crossbow. I have killed a couple of wild hogs, and helped to field dress them. We don't bring wild meat inside the complex because Francesca's Kitchen won't use it, but we cook it on our campfire and it tastes pretty good. We see wild dogs sometimes. My Dad says they are mostly pit bulls. We don't hunt them because my Dad says you have to eat what you kill and neither of us wants to eat dog meat.

"I know how to build a campfire and keep it going, at least in the dry season. I have never been camping in the rain. My Dad says that now he is a civilian he is never going to camp in the rain again.

"I have also learned a lot from doing volunteer work. I like to do technical things. Mostly I work as a helper for the maintenance crew. I go everywhere with the mechanics to hand them tools, clean up spills, clean and lubricate equipment, and do whatever else they need me to do. You would be amazed to learn how much machinery there is in this complex.

"I have learned a little about plumbing too. There is a lot more cleaning up involved with that. Plumbers say that there is nothing more important in a civilized society than dependable plumbing. I would hate to live in a dome with bad plumbing so they may be right about that.

"I am old enough now to be an electrician's helper, and I am really looking forward to it. My Mom is not too thrilled about it but I aced the test to be an apprentice, so she said I could give it a try.

"The reason I am learning how to do all these things is because when I grow up I want to live on Mars. I like the idea of being a pioneer in a place where people have never lived before. You wouldn't have to push anybody out of the way and you could take pride in what you are doing. I have already sent a letter of application to the Space Academy and they have put me on their waiting list."

In the domed communities of the Carolinas, children under five were not allowed outdoors. They looked forward eagerly to their five-year-old check-ups, hoping to gain access to the outside world.

Being outside the dome for the first time was exhilarating for young habitat dwellers. Wearing small oxygen masks, they ventured into another world. Running and playing on the wide clay avenues that separated domes from vines, they raced each other, chased each other, and ran circles around their parents. The first outdoor adventure was a rite of passage for the kindergarten set.

Children who turned five during wet weather received special treatment. They were all taken outside together soon after the rains ended, slipping and sliding in the unfamiliar mud. After they came back inside, their hands and faces were washed and they were given ice cream and cookies in the entrance area before being taken them home for baths. Their first, probably last, chance to play in the mud plus having an ice cream party almost made up for having to wait so long past their birthdays.

Megan went outdoors shortly after her fifth birthday, joyfully running around on the hard red clay, but Michael had asthma and was nine years old before he was allowed to join her. During long years of waiting, the boy had given a lot of thought to his future. When Michael finally stepped outside for the first time, the third-grader had decided that when he grew up he would live on Mars. Surely he would not be allergic to anything there.

As time went by and Michael continued to think about living on Mars, he put more effort into his studies, turning in all of his homework on time and spending hours on science projects. He read everything he could find about his country's European settlers and the Native Americans they displaced. Learning about the ways pioneers used what they found in the wilderness to produce tools, homes, food, and clothing, Michael decided to acquire some hands-on skills of his own.

In dome complexes, many tasks were assigned to adult and student volunteers. Seventh and eighth graders earned academic credit by volunteering two hours of labor two days a week, and received academic grades based on work ethic and productivity. High school students were expected to give more of their time, most of them doing so without complaint. No academic credit was given for paid employment, but many students found time for that too.

When he was twelve, Michael asked to be a helper on a maintenance crew. He followed mechanics and plumbers as they went about their work, handing them tools, cleaning up oil and worse, and doing whatever they told him to do. When he turned fourteen, he began working with electricians also.

At various times, he volunteered in almost every area of the complex, herding goats, slopping hogs, gathering eggs, mopping kitchens, clearing tables, sweeping walkways, trimming kudzu, pulping kudzu roots, and hosing down domes.

The summer before their junior year, Michael and his friend Dylan worked for pay at the brickworks several miles from the complex, ferried to and from their jobs in a company minicraft.

In a clearing next to a clay mine was an open-air work area devoted to preparing, mixing, and forming architectural brick. In another part of the clearing a large biomass furnace served as a kiln to fire the bricks. The boys cut and bundled kudzu growing around the brickworks, using a forklift to stack their bundles near the kiln. The clearing expanded as kudzu was cut and burned, making more room to stack the fired bricks. When the rains began, the brickworks abruptly shut down and was soon overtaken by kudzu.

During their junior year, Michael and Dylan worked for a short time as volunteers at the tannery, an odoriferous place hidden in a clearing five hundred yards from the complex. As few people wanted to work there, most of the tannery's jobs were handled by community service workers wearing ankle bracelets. The boys traveled to and from their work using agbelts, which they continued to wear while cutting kudzu around the clearing. That turned out to be the most strenuous job either of them had ever had, as well as the smelliest place they ever worked in, but they considered it worthwhile because for every two-hour shift at the tannery, each boy received credit for four hours' work.

At the tannery, huge nets were stored beneath a large platform twelve feet off the ground. The boys would pull out one of the heavy nets, spread it over the platform, and pile harvested kudzu on it as they worked. Every thirty minutes, a minicraft would appear and hover over the platform while Michael and Dylan hooked the corners of the net to its skids. After the mini left with its load of kudzu, they would get another net, spread it on the platform, and start cutting more vines. The boys got used to the smell and worked there until Megan pointed out to them that no amount of showering could eradicate the hint of the tannery that lingered about them, and the boys quickly decided to quit that job in order to improve their social lives.

For fun, Michael and Dylan marched in the drum and flag corps, playing complicated rhythms on their snares while Megan and her friends strutted around waving, throwing, catching, and twirling flags in perfect synchronization. During dry seasons the group practiced outside three times a week, marching up and down the avenue outside the education dome. In rainy seasons, they were allowed to practice once or twice a week inside the dome, but only if the drums were muffled and the flags weren't thrown too high.

chapter four:
the domeweavers

"Age is foolish and forgetful when it underestimates youth."
from "Harry Potter and the Half-Blood Prince"
by J. K. Rowling

uring the long dry summer of 2119, rising seniors throughout the Carolinas were asked to participate in a dome-raising project forty miles north of Greenville.

To lure Boeing's new maintenance and repair facility to their vicinity, the Cherokee County Planning Commission had promised to expand Gaffney's habitat area. As soon as site preparation for Gaffney's new habitat dome began, Boeing officials started buying large tracts of land for their new repair shop. The Boeing campus would include a landing strip, six hangars, and several sealed buildings. The maintenance/repair shop was projected to open in 2123, and the new dome must be ready for Boeing employees and their families by then.

Both Travis twins volunteered for this dome-raising trip, but for different reasons. Megan and her friends knew some of the Charlotte volunteers and were hoping to see them there. Michael had been accepted to the Space Academy as a habitat engineering major, and thought it would be good experience to help build an actual dome.

The local BMW complex offered its hovercraft fleet to transport the Greenville volunteers. This was a major camping trip. The crowded Gaffney habitat could not shelter hundreds of guest workers, and every group had to bring their own supplies. Sleeping tents, dining tents, oxygen generators, agbelts, and cartons of dried food were piled in each hovercraft alongside the passengers. Their hosts would supply water, Gaffney's community kitchens would deliver hot meals to them at the end of each day and whatever was in the cartons they brought with them would provide breakfast and lunch.

From high above, crystal dome communities appear to float like bubbles of foam on a green kudzu sea. The Gaffney complex would have presented that illusion if not for the acres of bare red clay and construction paraphernalia at one end.

The site had been prepared during a previous dry season. Kudzu had been harvested and the vines taken to huge drying barns. All that remained was a circular hedge of untrimmed and deep-rooted kudzu, abutting a 50 foot arc of the main habitat dome. As soon as the rainy season ended, the area was regroomed and a lethal dose of helium injected into the ground beside the kudzu hedge, which was then stripped of leaves in preparation for weaving. Even in death, the vines would remain attached to their heavy roots, anchoring the dome as the work progressed.

A long rainy season had just ended and construction needed to begin right away. Everything was in place. Inside the kudzu circle, dozens of limp balloons stretched hugely across slick red mud. Fully inflated, they would fit together like the sections of an orange to form a hemispheric mold for the weaving of the dome. The huge balloons, woven of kudzu fiber, were on loan from their manufacturer as a public service. They would be deflated and returned to Milliken for cleaning and storage when no longer needed.

Bundles of seasoned kudzu had been brought from drying barns and stacked high around the living hedge. Crews of student weavers would be trained and supervised by professional domeweavers. Ground crews led by county maintenance employees were staffed by adult volunteers.

When the kudzu dome was completed, a team of coating technicians would apply the first coating of Krystallizer, assisted by a group of Clemson students under the supervision of their materials science professors.

As the huge balloons filled and the mold began rising to its great height, crew leaders texed[6] instructions to the young volunteers. It was a breathtaking experience for Michael. Like most children growing up in Southeastern domes, he had begun agbelt training in the sixth grade and was at home in the air, but nothing had prepared him for a project of this size. In his excitement, Michael thought he might have an asthma attack, but biofeedback prevented it, and when the mold was ready, so was he.

Everyone gathered their vines and set to work, knowing that many lives would depend on their skill and attention to detail. The teen-agers labored with painstaking care as they hovered each day above the giant structure, sweating under their masks and agbelts, weaving for hours in silence under the clear gray sky. This was more than a construction project; it was a major rite of passage.

A Charlotte crew worked next to the group from Greenville. Michael was fascinated by one of their weavers, a girl who worked much faster than anyone else, making two trips to the supply area for every one of his, always returning with a huge bundle of vines. When a co-worker left and her workload increased, she never fell behind, doing the work of two people until a replacement arrived. Megan, stationed closer to the other group, traded places with her brother so he could get a better look.

Days passed, the great dome curved inward, and Michael moved ever nearer the graceful figure who floated lightly above her kudzu webs. While everyone else was building a place to

---

6 Texted

live, she was creating a work of art, her perfect triangles forming complicated patterns of geometrical perfection in a masterpiece destined for a tomb of living stone.

Michael wanted desperately to meet her.

At the construction site, supper was served in large tents freshly filled with habitat grade air. Masks and agbelts came off in the entranceways and the workers walked into the dining areas looking like themselves. After supper, most of them stayed awhile in the tents to relax, tex[7] friends back home, play video games, or simply talk about their day. The girls always had a lot to discuss, but most of the boys didn't say much except to complain that they were beat and could use some peace and quiet. Before leaving, they all deflated their dining tents and stored them in equipment lockers.

One night, after most of the dining tents had been folded and put away, the counselors gathered in the largest one. They were aware of conflicts due to what some called "too many people too close together." After a short discussion, someone proposed a system of all-male tents and all-female tents called single gender dining. Other ideas were presented, and it was decided to offer the additional choice of mixed gender dining, or "open dining," based on mutual interests. This information was texed to all the young workers, who immediately began texing[8] each other. Soon there were open dining tents for video gamers, chess players, robot builders, and other special interest groups. Surprisingly, there were few single gender tents.

Luna and Megan already knew each other. Two years earlier, their music teachers in the Greenville and Charlotte schools had arranged videoconferences so their students could get acquainted.[9]

---

7   Text
8   Texting
9   It was later learned that Mr. Parke had been conducting a long-distance courtship of the Charlotte teacher, and the videoconferences had been part of this process. The story came out when the teachers were married the following year.

The videoconferences had been a lot of fun, and the girls had kept in touch for a few months afterward. Now they and the rest of their musical friends were assigned an open dining tent halfway between the Charlotte and Greenville campsites.

The first time this group got together, they were almost too excited to eat. Virtual friendships were becoming real ones. Girls were hugging and boys were fist-bumping. Two boys brought harmonicas to accompany after-dinner singing, and Megan's friend Sharon unfolded a small stringed instrument she said was a ukelele.

By the time the food was delivered, everyone had arrived except Megan and Megan's dinner guest. Knowing there was room for another diner, Megan had texed all of her music class friends that she was going to invite the most studious and serious-minded person in her crew to join would surely be the rowdiest dinner group on the compound. They all told her to forget it, nobody like that would want to associate with them.

They were wrong. Megan had invited her brother.

Luna was the only person who knew that Megan was bringing Michael. When he stepped into the dining area with his sister, Luna thought, "He does look like the studious type, but that's to be expected. After all, he's been studying me for weeks." She was glad to see that he appeared to be quite normal. "If he's Megan's brother, he can't be too bad," she thought. "I'll try to be nice to him."

Luna had saved two seats for Megan and her guest, and soon a very nervous and awkward young man was sitting beside her. Now that he was inches from the object of his admiration, he felt too nervous to respond to her friendly greeting. He didn't have a clue what to say to her.

Michael stared silently at his hands, realizing they were clamped onto his knees as if to keep him from running away. He began to feel short of breath.

Luna decided to break the ice. "I hear that you want to build habitats on Mars," she said, leaning toward him. "Do you really plan to make Mars your permanent home?"

Michael looked toward her and nodded silently.

Luna smiled at him brightly. "I think that Mars would be a wonderful place to live, even better than the Moon."

Michael relaxed and began to speak.

Over the next few weeks, he and Luna cherished their time together. At lunchtime, they sat side-by-side on the ground beside the growing dome, lifting their masks to eat and drink. Every evening they ate together in the noisy dining tent, slipping out afterwards to stroll around the compound in the quiet darkness.

As the dome neared completion and workspace lessened, weavers began to depart, one or two groups going home each week until only the workers from Greenville and Charlotte remained, working side by side atop the nearly completed dome. When the time came for Michael's group to leave, Luna left her work to stand beside him until he boarded the big BMW hovercraft. Then she flew to the top of the dome and watched as the hovercraft rose and turned south toward Greenville, holding back her tears until it melted into the grayness of the sky.

PART TWO:

LIFE IN THE CRYSTAL DOMES

chapter five:
family matters

*"A pause in the day's occupations that is known
as the Children's Hour"*

from "The Children's Hour"
by Henry W. Longfellow

Upon returning from Gaffney, the Travis twins told their parents, John and Mary, about their dome-weaving experiences. The usually quiet Michael, in response to Mary's gentle prodding, was doing most of the talking while Megan listened quietly. "I'm responsible for this," she thought. "I hope I did the right thing, bringing them together."

This conversation, especially Michael's revelations about his feelings toward Luna, caused John and Mary to realize they could no longer postpone a serious talk with their children. Megan and Michael had never asked for details of their birth and adoption, accepting the simple explanation they had been given as young children. As young adults, they surely must have questions they were hesitant to ask. It was time they knew the whole story, and only their parents could tell them.

After dinner the next evening, the Travis family sat down together with all phones and computers turned off. Mary took a direct approach.

"Before we begin, please remember that you mean everything to your Dad and me," she said. "We held you in our arms moments after you were born. We were chosen by your birth mother to love and care for you. And we will always do that." Mary stopped speaking and John took over:

"Every month, several 'kudzu babies' are brought to this complex by families unable to take care of them. A family member signs a release and gives the child to a security guard. The children are taken care of by Mother Abigail and her staff until they are ready to go to new families. With human fertility rates the lowest in recorded history, people all over the US are waiting to adopt Greenville children, and most of the orphans are placed elsewhere. To avoid problems caused by too small a gene pool, it's better for adoptable children to grow up where their DNA profiles differ from the general population. But many find new parents here, just as you did."

"Thanks for the biology lesson, Dear," said Mary. She looked at her children. "Now I want to tell you about a girl from far away who came to South Carolina and fell in love."

"Mom, what are you getting at? Is this about Luna?" Michael was clearly upset. "What are you and Dad trying to tell me?"

"This is not about Luna." John's tone was very firm. "This is about your birth mother, yours and Megan's. Before either of you makes a commitment to another person, you need to know more about yourselves." John's tone softened. "Now apologize to your Mom."

"I'm sorry, Mom. I guess I'm just paranoid. I apologize." Michael was embarrassed. It wasn't like him to flare up like that.

Megan gave him a poke and a dirty look. She wanted to hear this great love story.

"I guess I took the wrong approach," said Mary. "What happened is that a family from northern Europe came to South Carolina in 2099 and leased a home in a private community near here. The parents were executives with a geothermal energy company and were here to start a joint venture with a local firm. They planned to stay for a year, two years at the most.

"Their youngest child, a sixteen-year-old girl, came with them. The daughter was home all day with a part-time tutor and a housekeeper. There were no other teen-agers in the community, and she got bored and started looking around for something to do. She wasn't supposed to leave the dome by herself, so she bribed a guard to let her out after her tutor left for the day. The housekeeper never kept up with her comings and goings, so – let's call her 'Ingrid' – went for a walk on the dome's perimeter road every afternoon. There were some young kudzu harvesters who worked there every day. One thing led to another, and she ran away with one of them."

"Wow," said Michael. "Not too smart, was she?"

Megan poked him again. "You will never understand women," she told him. She looked at her Mom. "Don't worry. I'll never do anything that stupid. Tell us more."

"It's hard to find people if they want to disappear into the kudzu," Mary continued. "'Ingrid' was missing for quite awhile. Almost a year later, I was working at the Table Rock Clinic when someone brought her there. She was sick, pregnant, and scared half to death. I brought her to Greenville and we notified her parents. She stayed with Mother Abigail until you were born. You know the rest."

"That's enough for tonight," said John, "unless you want to hear the part about your DNA."

"I suppose half of it came from far enough away for us to be able to live here," offered Michael.

"How about all of it?" his Dad replied.

The twins were all ears. "Tell us about it!" they said in unison.

John cleared his throat and prepared to give another speech:

"The kudzu trimmer went by the name of Boone. He had a forged ID which allowed him to pick up odd jobs in and around privately owned communities, but he stayed away from complexes like ours, where his past would have been more closely investigated. To this day, his real identity is unknown. According to the national DNA base, he has since fathered several other children, and each time abandoned the mothers before or shortly after the children's birth. Most of the other babies were given up for adoption also."

"Well, that's interesting," said Megan. "Not much of a love story."

"There's no record that he's been involved in criminal activity, but he is quite an adventurer. His aliases include Dave Boone, Dan Crockett, Sam Bowie, and my personal favorite, Lewis Clark. He seems to have descended from Cajuns uprooted from their Louisiana homes decades ago by the great Mississippi floods. A lot of Cajuns settled in northern Alabama, but none of the authorities in that region know who 'Boone' might be. There have been so many unrecorded births that it's hard to get much information about people.

"Megan, unless you also want to go to Mars, none of this should have any effect on you. We are your parents and always will be. You don't need to share this information with anyone until you are ready to marry and have children. Until then it doesn't matter."

John turned to his son. "You have already been accepted to the Space Academy as a Mars Colonization major. It is possible that your siblings or half-siblings might not be allowed to settle on Mars. Genetic diversity will be even more important there than it is on Earth or the Moon. After a few generations, people will no longer live in Earth gravity habitats. Your descendants will be Martians, with bodies shaped by Martian gravity. They might not be able to survive on Earth. The first settlers must be a healthy and diverse group of people so their descendants will be up to this challenge."

He smiled. "As far as finding the right mother for your own offspring, you seem to have that situation pretty well lined up already."

"Don't rush things, John!" Mary exclaimed. "They're still children themselves."

"Maybe, but they're older than their birth mother was when they were born. They're plenty old enough to know the facts."

Megan had a question. "So what happened to 'Let's Call Her Ingrid'?"

"Her parents returned to Europe about six months after she ran away," Mary replied, "telling their friends she was in an American boarding school. They had pretty much written her off by the time we found them and told them their daughter was alone in the world with two babies on the way.

"Her father wanted to disown her, but her mother was more forgiving. 'Ingrid' begged to go home, so he said she could come home if she would back up their boarding school story and tell nobody about what really happened. He also told her that as far as he was concerned her children did not exist. Her mother seems to have agreed with him on that point. 'Ingrid' would have to return alone."

"Tough choice," Megan commented.

"When you have children of your own, you'll realize how tough a choice it was," said Mary. "That was when she asked us to become your parents. As I told you, I was a Social Services nurse and one of my patients brought her to me after Boone deserted her. 'Ingrid' trusted me and knew you would be loved and cared for. In her own way, she really was a good mother who wanted the best for her children. Soon after you were born, her older brother came for her and took her back to Europe. We never heard from her again."

Mary smiled. "Now, Miss Megan, Mars is already taken, so if you want to go and be a pioneer on an asteroid somewhere, you had better stake your claim before someone else beats you to it!"

"No chance," Megan told her. "I'm going to stay right here and help clean up the Earth. Somebody has to do it, and it might as well be me. My DNA isn't going anywhere."

"Just so you know," said Michael. "I would never ever abandon my children."

"We know that, Son," said John. "Now it's time to adjourn. The new school year begins tomorrow and we'll all have a busy day."

Megan wanted to ask a few more questions, but they could wait. She felt physically and emotionally exhausted. Bedtime sounded like a good idea.

✿❧✿❧✿❧✿❧✿❧✿

chapter six:
luna in love

*"I'll remember you, long after this endless summer
is through"*

from "I'll Remember You" by Kui Lee

una came home at the end of the dome-raising project to find her parents waiting inside the main entrance of the Charlotte complex. During her absence, they had returned from an assignment and hoped to spend some time with their daughter before leaving on another one.

Charles kissed Luna on the forehead and took her duffel bag. Jenna hugged and kissed the girl, then took a step back, holding her at arm's length, and asked. "Sweetie, what's wrong? Aren't you glad to see us?"

"Hello Daddy. Hello Mama," said Luna. She took a deep breath. "I need to know something. How did the two of you feel when you first met each other?"

"What kind of a question is that?" asked her father, taking another step backward as if to keep from losing his balance.

"Charles, she wants an answer," said Jenna. She smiled at Luna. "He was tall, dark, handsome, and very polite. I liked him. Have you met someone?"

"Sometimes I feel as though my heart is floating in my chest," said Luna. "I forget to breathe. Then my heart starts pounding. I've never felt this way before."

"You need to see a doctor," her father told her.

"No she doesn't," snapped Jenna. "Your daughter's in love. I know the signs." She shot her husband a dirty look, and he strode off with the duffel bag.

"She's much too young to be in love," thought Charles. "She has a crush on some kid she just met. She'll get over it soon." Charles remembered how he felt when he first saw Jenna. "I'm not about to tell my daughter how I felt when I walked into that building and saw a knockout blonde," he thought. "Anyhow, that was different. We were both adults. Who does that boy think he is? What kind of line was he feeding her?"

That evening, Charles and his father-in-law were sent to watch a soccer game while Luna had a long talk with her mother and grandmother.

"Tell us how you met this young man," said Jenna.

"Mama, he was watching me. I knew that Megan was working on the project, but I didn't recognize her at first, with her mask on and everything. As we got higher up the dome, everybody was working a little closer together and I could tell who she was. I waved at her one day and she waved back. The next day she was farther away and this boy was in her place. He kept looking at me, so I didn't pay any attention to him. He wasn't like a stalker, but it was annoying just the same.

"I texed Megan and asked her what was going on. She texed back that it was her brother and he had a crush on me so she changed places with him. I thought it was kind of cute, flattering really, so I just let it go. I didn't even tell any of my friends about it. There's no telling what they would have said and I didn't want to be teased because some stranger was gawking at me."

"Then all of sudden you're in love with him?" asked her grandmother.

"Oh, Grammy, it wasn't all of a sudden. The counselors made some new rules about where everyone would eat supper, and

Megan and I were put in the same dining tent. She told me she wanted to invite Michael – that's his name – to eat with us and that she would vouch for his good behavior. What could I say? We would certainly be well chaperoned. So I told her I'd be nice to him and I was. We ate together every night for weeks and talked about everything in the world. We really got to know each other."

"And this was the first time you even knew he existed?"

"I didn't actually know him but I knew a little bit about him. I remembered Megan texing me a couple of years ago about her brother who wanted to live on Mars. At the dome-raising, when she said she was going to invite her brother Michael to eat with our group, I asked her about that and she told me he still feels the same way only more so. So I knew we'd have something to talk about. Which we did, and we had a pretty interesting conversation."

"Merciful heavens," sighed Grammy.

"Tell us more," said Mama.

"Michael is a wonderful person, very nice and very smart. He has a good sense of humor and he knows how to do almost everything. His friend Dylan was there too and Dylan told me all about him. They hang out together a lot, but he said Michael will have to go Mars without him.

"Michael told me that he and Megan are adopted. He said it's no big deal, but he thought I should know. He said his parents told him that they understand why he wants to live on Mars, even though they aren't real happy about it. His Mom and Dad have been everywhere and when they retired from military service they wanted nothing more than to spend the rest of their lives in one place, just settle down and raise a family. They came home from the war and adopted two babies. Now the babies are practically grown and I guess their parents would like for them to always live nearby, but Michael has his heart set on living on Mars."

"So now you want to go to Mars too? So much for living on the Moon," said her mother.

"I don't know what I want to do, Mama. I've never met anyone like him before. I just can't stop thinking about him. I don't know how this will work out. I don't know if we're really right for each other or if I would actually go that far from home. Mars is a lot farther than the moon and I don't know if I have what it takes to be a pioneer anyway. I just want to be with him. I miss him already and I just saw him less than twenty-four hours ago."

"Well, I guess we get the picture," said Grammy. "Suppose you tell us what else you did on your trip."

"Nothing of any importance except weaving a dome," answered Luna. "If you don't mind, I'd like to unpack now and reply to this tex I just got from Michael."

School started the following Monday. The next Monday was Labor Day, the day when Luna's parents were to leave for their new assignment. She walked with them to the zip station where they would catch a ride to Mega Mining's private airfield.

As they waited for the zipcar to arrive, Charles reached into his briefcase and pulled out a box wrapped in green paper and topped by a bright pink bow. When he handed it to Luna, she noticed a small tag that read: FOR LUNA - DO NOT OPEN UNTIL YOUR BIRTHDAY.

"What a beautiful package!" she exclaimed. "Are you sure I can't open it now?"

"We're sure, Sweetheart," said Charles. "And this is only part of your gift. The rest will arrive later."

Luna hugged her parents. "Thank you so much. I'm going to miss you on my birthday."

"We'll be here in spirit," said Jenna. "And don't even try to guess what's in that box."

"It's much too small to be a tiny spacesuit or even a little bitty agbelt," said Luna, teasing Mama by referring to her treasured childhood possessions. "I can't imagine what this could be."

"Call us after you open it at your party," Mama told her. "Here's our car. I hate to go so soon after you got home. We'll miss you, sweet Luna."

Charles and Jenna kissed their daughter goodbye and stepped into the zipcar. Luna waved at the car as it sped away, then turned around and headed for home with the mysterious gift in her purse.

chapter seven:
uncle phil

"Speak not but what may benefit others or yourself"
from "Autobiography"
by Benjamin Franklin

hilip Becker Jr. arrived unexpectedly a few days after Jenna and Charles left, showing up just in time for Luna's birthday. Poppy and Grammy were delighted to see their son. Phil Jr. never talked about his work. Luna knew only that her Uncle Phil worked for the government and traveled a lot. He dropped in every couple of years for a visit, sometimes coming when Jenna and Charles were there, sometimes not. A few weeks later he would leave as abruptly as he had arrived. He seemed to be working most of the time, but occasionally unplugged and relaxed with his family.

Luna was always glad to see her mysterious Uncle Phil. He had an air of freedom, despite the fact that he usually wore eyeware with a phone attachment and was constantly sending and receiving tex messages. Luna decided to speak privately with her worldly uncle. "Surely he can help me make a decision. He probably has more information about Mars than anyone else I know, and I'm sure he knows things that can't be found on the web," she thought.

Luna's grandparents gave a dinner party to celebrate her eighteenth birthday. When Poppy and Grammy left home early to see that everything was ready at the dining hall, Luna found an opportunity to talk with her Uncle Phil.

"Will you please wait and walk with me, Uncle Phil?" she asked.

Walking with her uncle a few minutes later, taking three hurried steps for every two of his long strides, Luna asked him, "Uncle Phil, have you ever been to Mars?"

"Why do you ask?" He slowed his pace and looked at her.

"I don't mean to be nosy, I just want to know if you have actually been there and what it's like."

"So what do you want to know?" he asked.

"What are the people like? How do they live? Are they stuck in a habitat all the time or can they get out and move around?"

"Well, everything out there is still pretty new. There aren't any malls or entertainment centers."

"You know that's not what I mean." Luna grabbed his arm and pointed to one of the benches that lined the walkway. "Let's sit down for a minute."

They sat down together and she continued. "You know that I might want to live out there some day. I'd like to learn about it from somebody who has actually been there. What kind of government do they have? Are there schools or churches or community centers or anything like that?"

"It's like any other new settlement, I guess," said Uncle Phil. "No children and nothing that you wouldn't find on any military base in an undeveloped area. Everything is in the planning stage." He turned and looked directly at his niece. "I've heard about your sudden interest in Mars. I never pictured you as a pioneer woman, standing by her man in the wilderness."

"Unless you've been in love, you couldn't possibly understand. I've never felt this way before and I don't know what to do." Luna was embarrassed to feel tears welling in her eyes.

Uncle Phil stood up and leaned toward his niece, reaching

down for her hand. He helped her up and they walked together in silence while he considered what to say next.

He decided to speak frankly: "Very few people have the coordination to combine the use of an agbelt with a complex weaving project as skillfully as you did. Even from a distance, young Mister Travis could see that you were strong, healthy, talented, and capable of working harder and faster than almost anyone else on that project. Perhaps unconsciously, he was attracted to the qualities in you that he'll need in a life partner and the mother of his children."

"What's so wrong with that?" Luna was offended by his tone. "We had to start somewhere. The better we got to know each other, the more in love we were."

"The point is this," Uncle Phil continued "loving each other is not enough. You, my sweet Luna, have not settled on a career, but your young man decided a long time ago to become a Martian pioneer and should have a wife as dedicated to that idea as he is. This needs to be as right for you as it is for him. It wouldn't be fair to either of you if you got to Mars and discovered you were in the wrong place. Neither of you would be happy, and if you had children, it would a bad situation for them too."

This wasn't what Luna wanted to hear. She started to protest, but her uncle gestured for her to be patient. They stopped walking and he kept talking. "I wish you would think about all of this very carefully. Be sure that spending the rest of your life on Mars is what you really want to do, not because you love a man who wants to go there and are willing to go with him, but because this is what you really want to do and you would want to go there even if you had never met him."

"Frank words," Luna said. "I asked for your opinion and I got it. Thank you, I think."

"I love you, little Luna, and I want you to be happy," replied her Uncle Phil. "That's my evaluation of your situation. What you do is up to you."

"Thanks, Uncle Phil. You've given me food for thought, and I'll definitely do some thinking later." She grabbed his arm. "Let's go. We're almost to the dining hall. I don't want to be late for my own party."

chapter eight:
birthdays

"Isn't it delicious to be a birthday child?"

from "The Birthday Child"
by Rose Fyleman

John and Mary Travis gave a big party for their children on September 10, the day before their eighteenth birthdays, sending dozens of teen-agers with lists in their hands on a massive Sunday afternoon scavenger hunt throughout the habitat. After everyone had returned with their collections, the partygoers gathered for an early dinner at Mama Francesca's Party Room, with dome-shaped birthday cakes and ice cream for dessert.

The green, blue, and white frosting on Megan's cake was designed to be a map of Earth's Eastern Hemisphere as it had looked before the oceans turned brown and the shrunken ice caps became a sickly shade of gray. Atop the cake stood a United States flag with a slightly smaller Greenpeace banner at its side.

Michael's cake, representing Mars, was frosted with dusky shades of red and brown and topped by United States and United Nations flags of equal size.

The scavenger hunt had been for items Mother Abigail needed for the children in her care. In addition, most of the guests had brought outgrown clothing and toys of their own to the party. Megan and Michael had never had a happier or more meaningful birthday celebration. After the party ended, several friends helped them take the donated items to the Children's Home.

The next morning, the Travis family ate leftover birthday cake for breakfast. John and Mary gave their children the texing minutes and Mall certificates they had asked for, and surprised them with hologram apps for their phones.

"These apps receive and send," explained John. "You can't make holograms, but you can receive them, pass them on and/or save them on a holostick. You can watch your holograms anywhere you have proper lighting and enough projection space."

"Wow, Dad," Michael said, "This is the coolest thing I've ever seen. How did you and Mom come up with such a great idea?" Megan added, "I would never have thought to ask for something like this."

"That's what surprises are for," said Mary. "One of these days your Dad and I will get a HoloCam for this family. We should have bought one a long time ago."

"I'm going to the library after school to check out a hologram movie!" Megan exclaimed. "Can this app show a movie in our living room?"

Michael had been reading the manual. "It can," he said, "but we'll all need magnifying glasses to watch it. Tell you what, I'll go with you and we'll pick out something together. We can show it in the courtyard."

"It won't project properly after dark," said John "and you'll never find time to watch a movie during the day. See if you can find something with one or two people in it that we can enjoy right here. How about a musician, a comedian, or a magic show?"

"We'll think of something, Dad," answered Michael. "We thank you both for a great birthday, both days of it." He and Megan kissed their parents good-bye and left for school.

Luna's birthday party, a quiet family gathering, was held

Monday night in the special events annex of her neighborhood dining hall. Her best friends, Ellie, Susie, and Abby, were also there, along with four generations of family members who lived in the Charlotte area.

After a meal filled with lively conversation ("The Becker family circus," muttered Uncle Phil), it was time to celebrate Luna's birthday.

The cake was brought out for everyone to admire. Luna was taken by surprise when she saw how it was decorated. "Oh Grammy," she exclaimed, "This is so beautiful!"

Luna's hemispheric cake represented a Crystal Dome, covered with white frosting thickly coated with rock candy crystals and crowned by a circle of toothpick lightning rods. A series of arcs cut from three-inch-thick cake layers was pieced together around its base, covered with frosting the color of Carolina red clay, and surrounded by a wreath of young kudzu.

There were no candles. Everyone opened the birthday apps on their phones, the guests sang "Happy Birthday," and when Luna blew out the candles on her phone, everyone else's candles were extinguished also.

The first gift she opened was the brightly wrapped package from her parents. Luna untied the bow and handed the ribbon to Grammy. Then she carefully removed the paper, folded it gently, and gave it to Grammy also. When at last she opened the box, everyone heard her gasp of astonishment.

Luna held up her new HoloCam. "I have wanted one of these forever," she told her guests. "If anyone knows how to use it, we can make hologram portraits of everyone here and no matter where I go, I'll have all of you with me."

"Let me see it," said Uncle Phil. "Your HoloCam should be fully charged and ready to use." He read the instructions, examining the device carefully. "It can also receive and project in real time, and store holograms sent by someone one else, including the sound. Everybody stand back and we'll give it a try." He pressed the HoloCam's power button, then took out his phone and texed briefly.

Suddenly Charles and Jenna appeared in the center of the room, singing the birthday song.

"Mama! Daddy! Thank you so much!" cried Luna.

"They can't hear you. Use this." Uncle Phil handed her his phone.

In future years, the holographic record of Luna's eighteenth birthday party was viewed many times by her children and grandchildren. The first entry in their 3D Family Album, it began with Charles and Jenna singing "Happy Birthday" to their daughter, patched seamlessly onto pictures made at Luna's party of the guests speaking individually before the camera. Her family would watch Luna's birthday party so often that they would take turns speaking in unison with her guests. They assigned the parts by age, the youngest child piping along with Luna's second cousin Lara, and the oldest person speaking in a dignified manner with Great-Aunt Marilyn.

Then they would watch quietly as their future matriarch opened the rest of her presents: A hologram projection app for her phone from Poppy and Grammy so she could carry on a live conversation while simultaneously sending and receiving holograms, eighteen hologram transmission hours plus a holochip titled "Mars Past and Present" from Uncle Phil, and eighteen hundred texing minutes from the pooled resources of her friends and relatives.

Although Luna's descendants largely remained silent during this time, whenever she exclaimed, as she often did, "I feel like a Queen," every man, woman, and child present would recite it along with her. In their eyes and hearts, a Queen she had been and always would be.

chapter nine:
luna's quest

"Things can never go badly wrong, if the heart be true and the love be strong"

from "Sweet Peril"
by George MacDonald

una took her Uncle Phil's words to heart. She made appointments with her pastor, her guidance counselor, Mega Mining's director of human resources, and her eighth grade English teacher.

"Maybe I'll gain some insight that will help me plan my future," she told her grandparents.

"Well that's an interesting selection of advisors," Grammy commented. "Let me see now – Reverend Gilder, Marge Davis, and John Williams – that should be enough to give you a pretty clear picture. So why do you need to talk with your old English teacher?"

"For a reality check," said Luna. "Ms. Weller never cut me any slack but she told me at the end of the school year that I was one of the best students she ever taught. She's not afraid to speak her mind and I can count on her for an unbiased opinion."

Poppy cleared his throat. "You haven't asked for our input," he said.

"I won't get an unbiased opinion from you or any other member of this family except maybe Uncle Phil, and what he said is the reason I want to talk with people who aren't related to me."

"You have a mighty cold-blooded approach to matters of the heart," was Poppy's reply.

"It's called the scientific method, Poppy. I already know what my heart tells me, and my blood is plenty warm enough. I know you and Grammy want to help me, but I need to go about this my own way." Luna smiled wanly. "I need to prepare some notes for my first appointment tomorrow. I'll be in my room if you want me for anything."

Throughout the conversation, Grammy had had sense enough to refrain from giving unsolicited advice. She looked at Poppy and put her finger to her lips to let him know the conversation was over.

In reality, May Becker was no happier than her husband about their granddaughter's eagerness to ask for advice from everyone but them, especially when their unmarried son was the first person Luna had consulted.

"Imagine her asking an old bachelor like Phil Junior for advice about love and marriage," May told her husband. She sat down on the sofa beside Philip and turned on the evening news.

Philip shrugged his shoulders and replied, "Luna isn't the first teen-ager we've ever had in this house. Dealing with her mother and uncle was no picnic either and they turned out all right."

Then the elder Beckers watched the news together while Luna stayed in her bedroom preparing for the following day's appointment.

Luna's first meeting was with Reverend Gilder. "Hello, Pastor. Thank you for taking the time to see me," she said when the church secretary ushered her into his office. "You've known me for a long time, so I hope you can help me with an important decision."

"It's always good to talk with you, Luna." he replied. "Have a seat and tell me what's bothering you."

Luna spent two hours with her pastor, choosing her words carefully in case parts of their conversation should appear in a future sermon. She left his office with a page of notes and several links to guides for engaged couples. Eventually she read them all, amazed at how complicated it could be for two people to determine their compatibility and plan a life together.

Immediately after school the next day she went to the office of her guidance counselor, Marge Davis, who gave her a warm greeting and then got right down to business. "Thank you for filling out those interest and aptitude tests I sent you. Let's pull them up on the big screen right now so we can look at them together."

"They were a bit tricky," commented Luna. "I've taken plenty of tests before but these were just a little bit different. I sometimes felt as though I had to choose the least wrong answer because there wasn't a right one."

"Psychologists who design these questionnaires do like to mess with people's minds, but the results can be quite revealing. Basically we are trying to find the best match for your interests, abilities, and personality, and do so within the context of available careers. Let's take a look and see just what Watson has for us." Mrs. Davis pressed a button and the first chart appeared on the screen.

Luna left the guidance counselor's office with so many links to career descriptions that she didn't have time to read them all before her next appointment. She simply printed out a two page list of possible career paths, each with a subset of occupations, and took it with her the next day when she went to see John Williams.

Luna knew that Director Williams, in his former position of Training Director, had arranged her flying sessions in the Mega Mining training dome soon after she moved to Earth. He had dropped by during her first session to say hello and ask if everything was all right. She remembered how pleasant and helpful her father's friend had been. Now the grown-up Luna was seeking his assistance in a far more important matter.

She spoke to the receptionist and signed the visitors' book. Before she could sit down, Director Williams entered the lobby and held out both hands to greet her. "I've heard wonderful things about you," he said. He led her to his office and pointed to a chair. "Please sit down and tell me what I can do for you."

Luna suddenly felt a little shy. "I want to know what career opportunities would be available to me with Mega after I finish college. I'm not sure yet if I'll prefer to work on Earth or the Moon, or maybe Mars if you plan to set up operations there."

Director Williams was all business. "What kind of career would interest you the most?"

"I like plants and I know a lot about medicinal herbs. Maybe I could work in plant biology or herbal medicine. Maybe growing things, improving yields by breeding new hybrids or developing new ways of growing food. Or I could be a chemist or chemical engineer and do research. I'm not really sure what I want to do, but I'd like to be breaking new ground instead of doing the same thing all the time."

"Let's start with Mars," the Director said. "Mega has no employees there and doesn't plan to have any in the foreseeable future. We are trading partners with the colonists, but all our people live here or on the Moon. Cargo ships go to and from Mars on a regular basis, and that's about it. Of course, there could be opportunities on Earth or Moon in all the areas you mentioned."

Luna had learned what she needed to know. She chatted for awhile with her father's old friend, telling him all about her birthday party and the gift her parents had given her, then thanked him and left, taking with her a list of links to careers available within the Mega companies.

Luna had begun to formulate a plan, and wanted Ms. Weller's opinion of it. The newly retired teacher had seemed flattered when responding to Luna's request for a meeting. The day after her conversation with John Williams, Luna knocked on Ruth Weller's front door. Her former teacher opened the door and invited her to come inside.

"Please have a seat, Luna. It's a treat to see you after all this time," she said. "My old students don't look me up too often, and sometimes I wonder how they fare after leaving my classroom. Would you like a cup of coffee, a cup of tea, or something cold to drink?"

"Coffee, thank you," said Luna. "It's good to see you again." She seated herself on an elaborately woven chair and set her purse on the floor beside her. "I was well prepared for high school English and anything else that involved writing after I left your class."

"That was the idea, my dear. Here's your coffee. I made a fresh pot just before you arrived." Ms. Weller handed Luna the cup and sat down facing her. "Now tell me how I can help you."

Luna hesitated a moment and then began:

"I've met someone I'm very attracted to. I might even marry him someday. But he decided years ago to become a colonist on Mars, something I had never imagined for myself. I don't want to lead him on, then ask him to give up his lifelong dream, and I don't want to end our relationship before I get to know him better. Right now I'd go anywhere with him, but maybe I won't feel that way five years from now. So I want to give our relationship more time and study for a career I can pursue anywhere - Earth, Mars, or the Moon – so I can find a job no matter how this thing works out."

She laughed nervously. "It's so sensible that I don't know why it took me so long to figure it out. My Grammy says I'm too much in love to think straight since I met Michael."

"He must be a remarkable young man for you to feel so strongly about him," said Ms Weller, "but I love that you have put so much time and effort into working through this, that you have done so in a thoughtful and systematic manner and especially that you value my opinion. I hope I get to meet this man some day."

The two women smiled at each other and chatted about other things as they finished drinking their coffee.

chapter ten:
megan

*"The whole world to think about, with very little time
for little things"*

from "For Arvia"
by Edwin Arlington Robinson

ike other kindergarten students, Megan was implanted with a data chip, fitted with eyeware, and taught to use these tools of learning. Upgraded annually with the touch of a wand, the chip was intended to be permanent. Eyeware, replaced periodically as she grew, was seldom brought home from school. Given the right password, any computer could retrieve, process, and store information in a student's data chip, ready to be downloaded later to a teacher's computer.

Upgrades were tailored to subjects a student would study during the coming school year, with courses so varied in the upper grades that the content was different for almost every student.

If a child's body rejected the initial implant, the chip was removed and the child's health monitored until a doctor approved another implant. Michael's first data chip had been removed, and he had been forced to study twice as hard as his classmates until his body was able to tolerate another one. Study habits acquired during this difficult period stayed with him for the rest of his life.

Sometimes Megan envied her brother's ability to apply himself to his homework. She was not studious by nature, and despite her data chip, seldom found her name on the Honor Roll with her brother's. One evening, after a particularly hard test, Megan complained about this to her mother. "You have good social skills," Mary told her. "Those are the most valuable if you wish to bring people together and persuade them to do important things."

"Are you saying that I should be a politician?"

"I'm saying that if you really want to save the planet, you need to be able to reach out to people and get them to listen to your ideas."

Megan's first impulse to say that she probably inherited these great social skills from the notorious "Boone," but realized just in time that her Mom might be annoyed, or worse yet hurt, by such a thoughtless remark. She took a deep breath and said nothing, smiling at her mother and thinking, "If having good social skills means knowing when to keep my mouth shut, I guess Mom is right. I guess I got my brown eyes from 'Boone' as well, because 'Ingrid's' were probably blue like Michael's." Megan decided to keep these opinions to herself as well.

Early in their senior year, there was a meeting of all Student Council and Senior Class officers. Around a large table sat Buzz Shealy, Ted Dawson, and Sharon Sullivan, the Student Council's President, Vice-President, and Secretary-Treasurer, respectively; along with Senior Class President Monroe Brown, Vice-President Michael Travis, and Secretary-Treasurer Sophie Lin. One of the items on the agenda was the selection of committee chairpersons for the year's activities.

The next day, Sophie asked Megan and Deeya to co-chair the Holiday Prom Committee. The girls accepted the challenge and posted a notice on the Class of 2120 Facebook page with a meeting schedule, a to-do list, and a request for volunteers. So many students responded that the first committee meeting had to be held in the school cafeteria.

Megan called the meeting to order while Deeya stood beside a whiteboard with a marker in her hand.

"Fellow Seniors," said Megan, "Let's ditch 'Robert's Rules' and do this roundtable fashion. Does everyone agree?"

A chorus of "Ayes" answered her question.

The meeting went quickly, Deeya's hand flying across the board as she neatly listed, diagrammed, and cross-referenced items under discussion. When the dust had settled and everyone indicated agreement with Deeya's chart, they took pictures of the board, storing the photos in their Winter Prom folders. The meeting adjourned and committee members scattered to their neighborhood dining halls to eat with their families.

Megan's family was waiting for her at their usual table. Her Dad stood up and gave her a hug. "Sit down, he said. "You look hungry."

"How did your meeting go?" asked her Mom.

"Pretty well," Megan answered. "It's a good thing Deeya and I are doing this together. She's much better organized than I am. Dylan even showed up and offered to build something. I'm sure we'll take him up on it once we decide what we need."

"Dylan hasn't got a date for the dance yet, but he told me that Jesse already asked Amy," said Michael. "I'm glad Jesse's going and taking Amy, but it would never have occurred to Jesse to tell me himself. Jesse lets Dylan do the talking for both of them. He's that way with everybody but Amy. When he's with her, the two of them put their heads together and never stop talking. It's as if the rest of us don't exist."

"Amy's the same way," replied Megan. "She usually keeps to herself and never has much to say. But she lights up when Jesse walks into the room. He may seem like the strong silent type to everyone else, but he falls all over himself when Amy smiles at him."

"Jesse's the only guy who gets a smile from Amy," said Michael.

"She never smiles at me or anyone else either. Dylan actually made a pass at her a couple of years ago and she just turned her back on him and walked away. Brrrr – a real cold shoulder." He grimaced. "That shook Dylan's confidence a bit, but he got over it. He told me he asked his Dad to help him – and this is a direct quote –'learn how to treat a lady.'"

Megan laughed. "Maybe his Dad taught him a little too much. There were girls falling all over him in Gaffney last summer, even the ones who delivered our meals. Every Sunday he went to a different church with a different Gaffney girl."

"Dylan did that so he could have a hot meal afterward at one of the local dining halls. Then he got another good meal Sunday night in the tent."

"That's typical Dylan," said Megan. "I wonder who he's going to take to the Prom."

"He hasn't thought that far ahead. By the way, he also told me that Jesse and Amy have been accepted to the Military Academy. They talked about it last summer when they were on ROTC maneuvers, and decided to enlist together."

"I think it's cute the way they have so much to say to each other," said Megan. "It must be love." She grinned wickedly. "You and Luna were just like that, jabbering at each other and nobody else."

Michael blushed. "We had to cover a lot of ground in a short time. By the way, I've got a little problem. I asked Luna to come to Greenville for the Holiday Prom, but her school is having one the same weekend and she wants me to go up there instead."

"We'll miss you," said his sister, "because if you know what's good for you, you'll go to Luna's prom and meet her parents. If you don't believe me, ask Mr. Murray. According to Dylan, his father knows a lot about women. He'll tell you the same thing I did."

Colonel Travis had heard enough. "What am I, chopped liver?" he asked. "I know a little something about women too. I can tell you what you need to know."

"Of course you can, Dad,' said Megan. "Please explain to your eighteen-year-old son that he needs to act like a grown-up."

"Man up and go to Charlotte," Michael's father told him.

Megan grinned wickedly. "Good work, Colonel," she said.

Michael groaned. "Luna has a ton of relatives in Charlotte: parents, grandparents, aunts, uncles, and cousins. I don't know if I can handle all that family."

His mother spoke up. "Well, you won't be bothered with any of them after you carry her off to Mars. Just go and get it over with. Tell her you'll go to her dance on condition that she agrees to come down here in May for your Senior Prom. Then your Dad and I can meet her too. I'm sure that Megan would be glad to share her room with Luna for a couple of nights. We'll all have a chance to become better acquainted."

"Please pass the butter," said Michael. He was quiet throughout the rest of the meal. After dinner, he sent a tex to Luna, accepting her invitation.

Megan had never had a serious boyfriend. Sometimes she liked one boy more than another, but never the same one for long and she never felt that she loved any of them. Some of her friends had developed fairly serious relationships, and it seemed to change them. Now even her shy, quiet brother was declaring himself to be in love and turning into a whole different person.

"I guess I'll know when the right man comes along," Megan thought. "I hope it's really the right person and not just some fancy talker with good looks and nothing else."

Her thoughts turned to her birth parents. "How could 'Ingrid' lose her heart to someone she barely knew and lose every bit of common sense along with it? How could her feelings be so strong that she would leave her family and the life she had always known to run away with him?" she thought. "How terrible it must have been for her when he abandoned her and their babies."

Megan often thought about the story that her parents had told her. Sometimes she was overcome with pity for the young girl who had given birth to her. Sometimes she felt sorry for herself, and resentful as well, wondering how any mother, even a very young one abandoned by her lover and estranged from her family, could reject her own children and disappear forever from their lives.

"How could she care so little about us that she would give us away? Why didn't she try to keep us, get a job, take care of us somehow?" Megan tried to imagine herself in "Ingrid's" place and still couldn't understand it.

"I need to talk with Mom about this," she thought. "She'll probably tell me that I'll understand when I'm older, but it's worth a try anyhow. I just don't know how to discuss these things with her without hurting her feelings. Mom was brave to do what she did, look after 'Ingrid' and take Michael and me to raise. She and Dad saved our lives and 'Ingrid's' too, and I would never say anything to hurt her."

Although Megan never found a way to talk with her mother about these feelings, it really didn't matter. As she matured into womanhood her understanding of life matured also, and such a conversation became unnecessary.

chapzer eleven: dylan

"We are the dreamers of dreams"

from "Ode"
by Arthur O'Shaughnessy

ylan Murray had also had his eye on Luna during the long days of dome-weaving, but when he saw the way Luna latched onto Michael and started talking about how great it would be to live on Mars, Dylan decided to let it go. Michael had always been shy around girls, but this one seemed to like him and Dylan could tell that Michael liked her.

"Let him have his big romance. There are plenty of other girls in this tent," thought Dylan. He looked around and muttered under his breath, "I sure wish I had brought my guitar."

Before the evening was over, Dylan's cousin Sophie had introduced him to several young ladies who had no interest whatsoever in going to Mars. He vaguely remembered them from the videoconferences. Juliana was lead singer for a band called The Charlotte Chickadees. Violet had just begun taking guitar lessons and asked him for advice. A couple of other girls were almost as interesting. Dylan would not lack for dinner companions during the final weeks of the project.

After he returned to Greenville, the biggest decision facing

Dylan was which girl to take to the Holiday Prom. Maybe he could invite Juliana to the December dance and Violet to the Senior Prom in April. Not to worry – there was plenty of time to make a decision. Of course there was the matter of transportation. Maybe he should ask a local girl instead.

Dylan, Jesse, and Sophie were first-generation Southerners. Their grandparents had brought Francesca's Kitchen to Greenville in 2085 at the urging of Doug Lawrence, a former customer who missed their cooking after he moved his fuel cell company from upstate New York into one of the old Paris Mountain bunkers.

While looking for potential employees at a job fair in Greenville's main dome, Doug Lawrence was told that the County Commission was seeking a new dining hall contractor. He asked the Chairman to contact the owners of Francesca's Kitchen and invite them to fly down for an interview. A phone call was made immediately.

Joe and Francesca Russo arrived in Greenville the following week, bringing with them several employees and a number of packages labeled Pantry. Before they slept, the group toured greenhouses, barns, pantries, bakeries, and kitchens. The next morning they took over the kitchen of the Administration Dome. At 1 PM, a group of city and county employees, including most of the security department, were served one of the finest meals they had ever eaten. At 7 PM, the mayor, city and county commissioners, and other employees and their families enjoyed an equally impressive dinner.

The Russo party left on a hoverjet the following day, receiving a texed offer while they were still in the air. A month later, bringing their children, several of their employees, and the employees' families, Joe and Francesca returned to Greenville. They all moved into temporary living quarters in one of the old bunkers, and Francesca's Kitchen began its reign in the Deep South.

Richard, Susan, and Patricia Russo grew up working with their parents in the restaurants. All of them learned to plan and prepare food for large numbers of people on a daily basis. Enjoying the challenge and the creativity, the girls decided to make Francesca's Kitchen their life's work. They both married co-workers and, with their husbands, helped to run the family business.

Richard had different ideas. In 2098, he earned a BS degree in Agriculture and became the complex's Manager of Animal Husbandry. In the habitat quality air of a dozen huge bunkers lived chickens, pigs, sheep, goats, a few border collies, and six watchful cats. This underground farm provided residents with meat, eggs, milk, and cheese, not to mention wool, leather, and a plentiful supply of fertilizer.

"I'm glad to be out of the kitchens and into the farm," Richard told his sisters. He grew a beard and took to wearing vintage overalls and an old straw hat he bought from one of the local kudzu divers. When offered the position of Director of Agriculture, he turned it down because it was a desk job. He then bought a pair of vintage boots and a couple of red bandanas.

Sean and Susan Murray's sons, Jesse and Dylan, and Steve and Patricia Lin's daughter Sophie were born in 2101 and grew up in kitchens just as their mothers had. The children also spent a lot of time helping their Uncle Richard, gathering eggs and doing other chores in the underground farm.

In 2110 Papa Joe decided to retire and become a volunteer in the barns. He bought some old overalls and a leather hat from Richard's kudzu-diving friend and was seldom seen in the kitchens again.

Papa Joe and Richard sometimes took Jesse and Dylan and their friends camping, accompanied by a few parents and security officers. Dylan's best friend Michael and his father were always part of the group. John Travis, who had hired and trained all the current security officers, was highly respected by everyone. He believed it was important for young people to get away from the comforts of the dome and learn some survival skills. Sometimes Mary would come along, bringing Megan, Sophie and a few of their friends. As it turned out, most of the volunteers who later took part in the dome-raising project had been on at least one of these camping trips.

Their usual campsite was a granite outcropping on a mountain near the North Carolina border. The campers would cut back any kudzu encroaching on the clearing and then build a fire to cook their supper. They would sit around it for hours, feeling a bond with generations of people before them who had gathered around an evening fire for comfort and companionship in a dangerous world. After supper, Dylan would play his guitar and they would sing and talk as the fire slowly died down. When the embers were extinguished, the campers would inflate their tents and sleep in habitat-grade air while heavily armed security officers stood watch through the night.

Sometimes a local kudzu diver would approach the group, wanting to do a little business. Campers carried small items for barter in case a diver showed up with something interesting. Michael was always on the lookout for small pieces of scrap metal that he could reshape at the forge behind the Service Dome. When he had nothing of his own to barter with, he used his pocket money to buy powdered eggs and powdered goat's milk to trade. Jesse accumulated quite a few hand tools over the years by trading all of his outgrown shoes and most of the toys he had played with as a child. He gave some of the tools as Christmas gifts to his father and uncles and kept the rest in his closet. Although Dylan wasn't usually into trading, he once swapped a new pair of socks for a harmonica, and another time he swapped an old guitar for some beautifully woven baskets to give his mother for her birthday.

Dylan and his friends accepted their way of life. Crowded into a dome, wearing supplemental oxygen to venture outside, and accompanied by armed guards on a simple camping trip - this was their reality. They knew that life had once been simpler, but they got on with their lives and didn't complain about uncertain weather and other petty annoyances.

Earth's temperate zones no longer had four predictable

seasons with precipitation scattered throughout the year. The climate was so unstable that no meteorologist could predict next week's weather with any degree of accuracy. The weather changed from wet to dry several times a year. Wet seasons arrived almost without warning and lasted for weeks or months. Dry seasons also began abruptly and seemed to last forever, the wide clay avenues so parched that the slightest disturbance stirred up clouds of fine red powder that lingered in the muggy air above the domes, dusting the crystals and collecting thickly in the crevices. Dome dwellers spent their days in a dim pink twilight until the rains came again, driven by gusting winds that scrubbed the crystals clean. Even the deep-rooted kudzu slowed its spread during a long drought, its leaves dangling limply in the hot unmoving air, then sprang into exuberant growth when the rains began.

The 2119 summer dry season lasted until the Gaffney dome was completed and coated with Krystallizer. Coating would resume during the next dry season, followed by applications of KrystalGrow during dry seasons for at least two more years. The crystals would meld into a thick layer of solid rock whose sparkling surface would give no indication of its incredible strength.

During the heavy rains of September and October, there was little travel in the Carolinas. There were no camping trips. The brickworks and the tannery shut down, disappearing beneath the kudzu. People ventured out only when absolutely necessary. Security officers wore ponchos over their helmets and agbelts as they made their rounds, floating wraithlike in the rain and fog.

In Greenville, Dylan and Michael drove a rambunctious herd of billygoats through the slippery red mud surrounding the complex. The goats were reluctant at best, preferring to be in a dry barn eating dry food, but their services were needed to prevent kudzu from overtaking the domes.

Dylan fashioned raincoats for the goats from old ponchos and tethered the strangely dressed animals to the thickest stems he could find. The goats soon learned they were not allowed to go back inside until they had eaten every leaf they could reach. Dylan took pictures of the goats and posted them on his Facebook page.

While Papa Joe was enjoying his retirement by herding goats and teen-agers, Mama Francesca was not ready to leave the business that bore her name. She had turned over day-to-day management to her daughters and sons-in-law, but insisted on having the final say on everything. Taking up pottery as a hobby, she commandeered a small oven in the main kitchen as her private kiln. Her sons-in-law set up her potter's wheel in a corner of the largest pantry.

Mama Francesca had never been happier. She went to her place of business each day, keeping an eye on everyone and everything, spending hours making pitchers and bowls to use in the dining halls. Every evening her large family gathered around the table with her and Papa Joe and discussed the day's events. As far as she was concerned, life didn't get any better than this. Eventually her grandchildren would take over the business, and their parents would see to it that the name would always be Francesca's Kitchen.

Francesca's daughter Susan knew that her sons had other ideas, but saw no need to mention this to their grandmother. Jesse had his heart set on a military career, and had been accepted to the Military Academy. "As for Dylan," Susan thought, "all he seems to care about is messing around in the kudzu or playing the guitar. After Jesse and Michael leave for college, what will Dylan do? Maybe he'll become an itinerant carpenter and travel from job to job with his guitar and his toolbox."

It was true that Dylan couldn't work up much enthusiasm for running a large food service business. On the other hand, he thought it would be fun to someday have a small coffee shop where he and a couple of back-up musicians could entertain the customers. He had talked about that in the dinner tent with Violet and Juliana, both of whom said it sounded interesting.

Months later, when Dylan mentioned this idea to Megan, she said, "It sounds like a good idea to me. When I need a break from saving the planet, I'll drop by for a cup of coffee and some live music. You need a catchy name for the place though. I think you should call it 'The Goat Coat Café.'"

chapter twelve:
uncle Richard

"All things come to him who waits."
President Woodrow T. Wilson

Richard Russo enjoyed training and supervising the employees and volunteers who fed the animals, gathered eggs, milked nanny goats, and herded billygoats outside to graze. He was proud of the goat herd, a healthy blend of several dairy breeds strengthened by frozen goat sperm brought by Papa Joe from the Russo farm when the family moved to Greenville.

Goats have a special importance in the crystal dome complexes. Nannies spend all their time in the barns, breathing habitat air, eating food-grade kudzu, and producing high quality milk. Most of the time, billies are with them, enjoying uncontaminated food and air, but their services are also required outdoors. In the Greenville complex, groups of billygoats were taken out on a rotating schedule to keep the clay avenues free of vines.

Although many aboveground structures are hidden beneath the kudzu, crystal domes and their encircling avenues are always kept free of vines. While it isn't hard to remove an occasional tendril from a glass or spinel dome, the jagged surfaces of the crystal domes are much harder to care for. They are beautiful to look at and economical to build, but digging the relentless kudzu from their crevices is like trying to clean the teeth of a thousand alligators.

The goats performed a necessary service. A herd of hungry goats doesn't allow a single vine to get near a crystal dome. Rain or shine, there are always a few goats tethered outside.

Growing up in Greenville, Richard had thought wistfully about his grandparents' farm in upstate New York. The happiest days of his childhood had been spent there, working in the greenhouses with his Nonna and helping Grandpa Tony care for the livestock.

A country boy at heart, Richard had never felt at home in the urban environment of the crowded domes. In his younger years, he had not lacked for feminine company, but had never met anyone who shared his interests. He finally withdrew from the social scene and become everyone's bachelor friend, then everyone's bachelor uncle.

In October 2119, when Richard was in his mid-forties, his parents asked him to accompany them on a trip to New York State. This was not an ordinary visit. Papa Joe's aged father had just passed away, and although the rainy season was at its height, they were determined to attend his funeral. Adding to their distress, Papa Joe's stepmother wanted to sell her share of the family farm. Richard's help was needed to determine the property's value. Family friend Doug Lawrence offered to provide transportation, making room for the Russos on his private hoverjet.

Papa Joe's mother, Richard's beloved Nonna, had been gone for twenty years. Fifteen years ago Grandpa Tony had married Vera, his housekeeper. Vera, a widow about the same age as Papa Joe, had moved in shortly after Nonna passed away, living upstairs in the big stone farmhouse with her two teen-age daughters. After the girls grew up and left, leaving the old farmer alone with his housekeeper, getting married seemed the logical thing for Grandpa Tony and Vera to do. Joe and his brother Dom approved of their father's decision, knowing big-hearted Vera would always take good care of him.

Vera and her stepsons would each inherit a one-third interest in the farm. She wanted to cash out her share and move to Arizona. Joe and Dom felt that a face-to-face meeting would be the best way for them to work things out. Doug Lawrence's lawyer would help them.

"I'm glad you're coming with us, Richie," Mama Francesca said to her son. "And it isn't just because you can help Papa with the property issues. You were very close to your Nonna, and I was close to her too." She smiled at Richard. "I guess I need you with me mostly for moral support. Vera and I went to high school together, and I've never felt comfortable having a former classmate as a mother-in-law. I'm afraid I've never made much effort to be close to her."

"I understand, Mama," Richard told her. "To me, Vera has always been more like an aunt than a grandmother, and besides I really haven't seen her very often. This is hard for everybody." He patted his mother's hand. "You and I will be there for Papa. I'm sorry that the others couldn't come too, but we'll help him through this."

Richard was more right than he realized. Mama Francesca would have preferred to remain at home with her potter's wheel and kiln, but she knew her place was with her husband. She and Richard would lend their support to Papa Joe, who had been grieving over his father's death and now had this property matter to deal with.

From Albany International, Richard and his parents took a zipcar to the North Albany Dome where Tony Russo had lived for the past ten years with Vera and her daughter Stella. The two women greeted them tearfully at the zip station and together the group traveled on moving sidewalks to Stella's apartment building.

Back home, Richard's sisters were glued to their phones as their mother kept them posted on everything. In Albany, the following day was devoted to preparations for that night's wake and the next day's funeral. Dom and his family arrived in time for everyone to go together to the wake at the Knights of Columbus Hall.

The next afternoon, a Funeral Mass was held in Albany at the parish church, followed by a reception in the church's fellowship hall. In Greenville, St. Mary's Church was filled with Papa Joe's friends as a hologram of his father's funeral service was shown in real time behind the altar rail. Father Clancy and a visiting priest stood on either side of the holographic funeral to serve communion to members of the Greenville congregation. A reception was held later in Francesca's Kitchen's largest event room.

Later that night, Susan and Patricia brought their families up to date on events in Albany. Mama Francesca had been keeping them fully informed. "You'd think Mama's fingers would have fallen off by now," Susan whispered to her sister.

Patricia frowned. "Don't be disrespectful," she hissed.

Patricia tapped a spoon against her glass for attention. "Mama and Papa will be home next week," she announced. "Richard will be staying for awhile to see everything goes smoothly while changes are being made."

"What changes, Mom?" asked Sophie.

"Uncle Dom and his family have been working the farm for the past ten years. Uncle Dom wants full ownership now so he can pass it on to his children." Patricia answered. "They're trying to figure out the best way to do it. Everything has to be appraised first and it's all very complicated." Dylan spoke up. He had gotten some texes too. "Uncle Richard says there's nothing there anymore except the house, an old barn where they keep the mowers, and a couple dozen greenhouses. Grandpa sold the goat herd before he moved to the city, and when Uncle Dom took over he sold the chickens too. Uncle Richard says the greenhouses are a big money-maker and he thinks Mister Lawrence can help find some financial backing for Uncle Dom."

"Your grandmother says Vera wants to cash out her share of the farm," said Susan. "Apparently she and Stella are going to move to Arizona. Vera's daughter Rose lives in a commune near Sedona and wants them to move out there with her."

Sean laughed out loud. "The people who run those places can smell money clear across the continent," he said. "Whoever runs it won't give Rose a moment's peace until she persuades her mother to go out there with a fistful of cash to keep the place going until the next patsy comes along."

Susan started laughing too. "Papa would sell his share to Uncle Dom for a dollar down and a dollar a week if he had to, but poor Uncle Dom will still have to rake and scrape together a big pile of money so Vera can take it to Arizona and use it to support a group of hippies."

Jesse and Dylan began to laugh, Sophie got the giggles, and then everyone at the table joined in. Patricia and Steve tried not to laugh but couldn't help themselves. They knew Vera had taken good care of Grandpa Russo and they loved her for it. But Sean's description of Vera crossing the continent with a fistful of cash to rescue a hippie commune in distress was just too much. Releasing the tension of the past few days, they all laughed until they cried.

Finally Steve wiped the tears from his eyes. "We should be ashamed of ourselves. We have no respect for our elders."

"You're right," said Susan. "Shame on us. Vera does need a change of scene. I doubt she's ever been out of New York. And maybe Sean is wrong. Maybe the commune would be a great place for her to live, and maybe they don't need her money, but I still believe that someone needs to check out the people who run it and try to talk her out of going there if anything looks suspicious."

"She wants to be with Rose, and Rose happens to live in a commune," said Patricia. "It's none of our business what she and Stella do now."

Steve, the chief financial officer of Francesca's Kitchen, spoke again. "Vera is a member of our family and we need to look out for her best interests. The lawyers will see that she doesn't get all of her money at once. Properly invested, it should provide a comfortable income for the rest of her life."

"Well, we'll see what happens," said Patricia, "but none of it will happen overnight. Papa says it will take at least another week for the reading of the will, appraisal of the property, and working out the legal details of Uncle Dom buying Vera's share. Richard is staying at the farm to look things over, but they need to have at least one state-certified appraiser look at it before everyone can agree on how much the place is worth."

"Time to adjourn," said Sean. "Some of us have to get up early tomorrow."

A week later, Doug Lawrence's hoverjet descended to the Greenville landing area. Mama Francesca and Papa Joe were met by security officers carrying large umbrellas and hustled into the main dome, to be greeted by Steve and Patricia.

The women hugged and the men shook hands. "Welcome home, Mama. Welcome home, Papa," said Patricia. "Where's Richard?"

"It's good to be home," said her mother. "Your brother has unfinished business. He'll be in New York awhile longer."

"What kind of unfinished business?"

"Richard is courting Stella," said Papa Joe. He grinned widely. "He's trying to get her to change her mind about moving to Arizona with her mother. Rose is already there and Vera will be fine without Stella. Rose would probably be glad to have her mother to herself for awhile anyhow."

"Good for Richard," said Steve. "More power to him. What does Stella have that our local ladies don't?"

"She's a farm girl," Mama Francesca explained. "After Vera's first husband died, Vera and her children moved in with Vera's parents. Stella doesn't remember living anywhere except her grandparents' farm and the Russo farm until she married and moved to Albany. She got such a good job with the New York State Department of Agriculture that she stayed in Albany even after her divorce, but she isn't really a city girl at heart. Richard is trying to talk her into moving down here."

Mama Francesca looked around for a place to sit. "Your brother is crazy about Stella. He even shaved off his beard. He's trying to convince her that Greenville is every bit as good as an Arizona commune and the food here is a whole lot better."

"That's very interesting, Mama," said Patricia. "Here's a bench. Let's use it."

They sat on the bench together as the men continued homeward with the luggage.

"It's good to have you back, Mama," Patricia continued. "All of us have missed you terribly. Now let's rest here for a little while and you can tell me more about Richard and Stella."

After a heart-to-heart conversation, the women got up from the bench and walked the rest of the way home arm-in-arm.

On Thanksgiving Day, Richard and Stella stood together before a Justice of the Peace in the Albany County Courthouse. Vera stood behind them as they recited their marriage vows, dabbing tears of joy from her eyes.

chapter thirteen:
winter holidays

"'Tis the season to be jolly."

Old English Carol

he Saturday after Thanksgiving, Dylan was trying to write a song. He had been informed only the day before that this was required of him.

"We don't need you to build anything for the Winter Prom because Deeya and I found plenty of props stored under the bleachers in the school gym," Megan told him, "but it would be nice if you could write a little something to be played and sung when the Queen and her Court come out. Remember that our theme is 'A Midwinter Night's Dream.' I can't think of any song I've ever heard that fits it."

"I offered to do a little physical labor," he answered, "not write an original piece of music, for Pete's sake! Besides, I thought we were using a deejay."

"We are," Megan replied smoothly, "but I know you want to help and a special song would be perfect for what we're doing. Besides, it should be easier than all that lifting and hammering, and you know you're good at this sort of thing. So, how about it?"

Dylan shrugged. "Sure, I'll do it."

Then he turned away abruptly and stalked off thinking,

"What makes her believe that writing a song is easy? What does she know about anything anyway? How am I going to write a song about 'A Midwinter Night's Dream' for Pete's sake? This is what happens when girls are in charge of something."

So now it was Saturday and Dylan had a song to write, with no inspiration other than getting Megan out of his hair. He cued up a little Shakespeare on his eyeware and tried to find a line or two he could plagiarize.

"I need to write in my key," he thought, "because I just might end up singing the thing and playing it too, unless she already has a vocalist and keyboard player lined up. I should have asked her a few questions when I had the chance, but I'm not going to go looking for her now. She'll show up sooner or later and I'll ask her then."

While Dylan was struggling with his assignment, Deeya was happily working at her computer, designing capes for the Prom King and Queen. When she was done, she texed Megan to meet her at their favorite Smoothie Bar.

Megan, bringing the crowns and tiaras she had found in a storeroom, found Deeya waiting for her at the Smoothie Bar. They looked over Deeya's designs, drank their smoothies, and went shopping for fabric. The old capes needed to be replaced. After visiting a couple of stores the girls realized they didn't have enough money for the quality of material they wanted.

They stood in the center of the mall, trying to decide what to do next. "Let's try a thrift shop," suggested Deeya. "You never know what you might find in one."

At the third thrift shop, the girls discovered three practically new bridesmaid's gowns in the icy shade of blue they wanted. The clothing held enough fabric to make capes for the royalty and sashes for the ladies of the court. They bought the gowns and carried everything to Deeya's home, then Megan said goodbye and headed homeward too.

When she got there, Michael was standing outside waiting for her, and he didn't look at all happy. "What did you say to Dylan?"

he demanded. "He and I were supposed to shoot some hoops this afternoon. I didn't hear from him and got no answer when I texted him, so I went by the Murrays' place and found him sitting on his bedroom floor. He had his eyeware on, reading Shakespeare, and he was picking random notes on his guitar and mumbling about how he wished some people would make up their minds about what he's supposed to do. I asked him what was going on and he told me what you said."

"Hello to you too," said Megan.

Michael pointed a finger at his sister. "It isn't 'some people' that got Dylan all in a tizzy, it's one person and her name is Megan. He offered to help with the Prom but he wasn't counting on having to write a song."

Megan stood her ground. "You mean *you* weren't counting on him having to write a song. Dylan writes stuff all the time and you know it. He was just displaying a little artistic temperament for your benefit. He'll get over it, and he'll come up with something perfect for the Midwinter theme. You'll see. Too bad for you that he'd rather be doing something related to his music career than throwing a basketball around."

"I think he's scared of you," said her brother. "I don't know what this hold is that you have over him."

"You're exaggerating now," Megan answered. "And I'm sorry if I upset anybody. I guess I'm in a bit of a tizzy myself. All this stuff about 'Let's call her Ingrid' and 'Look at her Luna' has me a bit unsettled too. And you can't even go to your own Winter Prom because it's the same day as 'Look at her Luna's' and you have to go to hers instead. Which I completely understand and agree with, but still – well, you know what I mean."

"Okay Sis, we'll call a truce. How about you go and shoot some hoops with me?"

"Sure," Megan said, laughing. "Just for a little while though. We don't want to be late for supper. You know how grumpy the Colonel gets when that happens."

Friends again, the Travis twins headed for the park together.

As usual, the weeks between Thanksgiving and Christmas passed quickly. A school concert, a church cantata, and a surprise wedding reception for Richard Russo and his new bride after their arrival from New York State punctuated the holiday season.

Later, Mary Travis told her husband that the Russos' party was the only wedding reception she had ever attended where the main topic of conversation was fish.

"There was Stella, looking so beautiful and happy, and the only thing Richard seemed to be really excited about was those fingerling trout he brought back with him," she said. "As if anybody cared about a bunch of fish when the most important thing he brought home was standing right next to him!"

"Dear, don't be so hard on the man," John told her. "Stella was every bit as excited about the fingerling trout as he was. After all, it was her idea and she had to pull a lot of strings to get them."

"Well, at least we know they have something in common," Mary replied. "When they have learned all there is to know about each other and run out of things to talk about, they can always talk to each other about their little fish and wonder how they'll turn out when they grow up."

John laughed. "Tasty, I hope," he said.

The last school day of 2119 was Wednesday December 20. There were signs that the rainy season was ending, which couldn't happen too soon for most people. Even in a crystal dome, it is possible to suffer from cabin fever when the sun never shines and the rain never stops. Dylan finished his song, Sharon offered to sing it, and Mr. Parke said he would accompany them on the keyboard.

Dylan eventually asked a couple of girls to go to the Prom with him, but they already had dates. Earlier, Megan had brushed off a couple of invitations, saying, "Ask me closer to time. I'm so busy planning this event that I don't know if I'll even have time for a date." Eventually she and Dylan took pity on each other and decided to go to the Prom together.

Sharon Sullivan, who had left for home Wednesday afternoon,

returned on Saturday with her brother Alec, who was on his winter break from a Virginia boarding school. Their father, known to everyone as Trader Bill, brought them to Greenville in his hovercraft.

Alec took Deeya to the prom, Sharon was escorted by Monroe Brown, the senior class president, Jesse and Amy went together as usual, and Sophie brought Omar, a Furman student who worked part-time in Francesca's Kitchen. Everyone missed Michael, but he couldn't be in two places at once.

The Winter Prom was a big success. All of the seniors attended, with or without dates. Most of the juniors and a sprinkling of underclassmen were there also. Monroe was chosen King and a cheerleader named Peggy was chosen Queen. They looked suitably regal in their crowns and capes.

Amy and Sophie were among the Ladies of the Court, much to their surprise. Dylan was not surprised a bit, as he and Jesse had done quite a bit of lobbying among their friends. Sharon, also a Lady of the Court, was delighted by the honor and felt sure Monroe was responsible. The Ladies all looked quite glamorous with their sashes and tiaras, and lots of pictures were taken.

Sharon sang Dylan's song "Midwinter Romance" while the King and Queen danced together and the other Court Ladies danced with their escorts, then the deejay took over and the dancing continued well into the night.

After the Prom ended, Dylan and his friends stopped briefly at a Smoothie Bar, then walked to Deeya's home, where Sharon and Megan were going to spend the rest of the night.

Dylan surprised Megan with a goodnight kiss, then hurried home alone.

"I sure didn't see that coming!" Monroe exclaimed.

Alec laughed. "That makes two of us. The girls will have plenty to talk about at their sleepfest. I'm sure I'll get an earful from my sister tomorrow."

Monroe lived near the Travis family, where Alec and his father were staying, so the boys left together, hashing over the evening's events as they walked homeward through the night.

Home-schooled through eighth grade, Alec and Sharon had both planned to attend high school in Greenville, but when Alec refused to have a data chip implanted, declaring he was "quite capable of learning without becoming a cyborg," the Board of Education refused to admit him. His sister stoically accepted her implant, moved in with Deeya's family, and melded into the public school environment. With Colonel Travis's help, Alec was later accepted by a military boarding school in Virginia, where he was given plenty of time to study and little time to do anything else. He often wondered what life would have been like if he had accepted that pesky little chip like everyone else.

When he reached the Travis home, Alec let himself in with Megan's key, quietly locking the door behind him. He slept in Michael's room that night, falling asleep to the sound of his father snoring gently in Megan's room nearby, and was still sleeping the next morning when Trader Bill showed John and Mary how to use their new HoloCam.

Trader Bill had heard about a camera shop in Raleigh going out of business and picked up some holographic products at a deep discount. When he called Mary and offered to let her have a top of the line camera at the same price he had paid for it, she was almost beside herself with joy. Mary and John went to the prom as chaperones, taking Trader Bill in the role of photographer, where he used the Travis family's new HoloCam to take pictures at the prom, including a cameo of his own daughter singing "Midwinter Romance."

Alec finally woke up and followed the sound of music into the living room, where he was stunned to see a miniature version of his sister singing at the Prom, with a tiara on her head and a pale blue sash draped across her red gown. "Wow!" he exclaimed. "Good morning, everybody. What's going on?"

"Santa Claus came early," said Trader Bill. "He asked me to bring a little surprise for Megan and Michael, and there might be one under our Christmas tree too. Don't mention this to your sister or your mother. Let them be surprised."

"Sure Dad," Alec replied. "This is really cool."

The four of them drank their coffee that Christmas Eve morning, watching the Prom's King and Queen dance together to Dylan's song, interspersed with a shot of Megan and Deeya jumping up and giving each other high fives.

"Were we ever that young?" Mary asked rhetorically.

The men laughed, Alec smiled, and the miniature dance continued in the Travis living room.

Later that day, the rain stopped and the sun came out again. Alec and Sharon left for home and Michael returned from Charlotte, beaming with happiness because Luna whispered to him as he left that he had won the hearts of her parents and grandparents just as he had won hers.

Furman opened its campus to the public for a Christmas Eve sing-along around the big fir tree at the center of the campus, and Santa Claus showed up when the singing ended to hand out candy canes.

On Christmas Day, Michael and Luna spent much of the afternoon in a holographic conversation, while Megan and her parents took a walk outside the dome, enjoying the sunlight as they struggled through the sticky clay in their high rubber boots. Finally, Megan took off her boots and walked barefoot through the red mud, daring her parents to do the same. When they got home, Michael had finished his conversation with Luna and was rereading the HoloCam manual.

On the way to the dining hall for Christmas dinner, Megan and Michael walked together a few paces behind their parents. When she told him about Dylan's kiss, he smiled. "You really do have power over him, don't you?"

"It's the Christmas season," she replied testily. "People do strange things during the holidays."

On December 26, a mob of excited five-year-olds played in the muddy avenues around the domes. Covered in red mud from head to toe, they were soon brought inside for their ice cream party, then taken home for baths.

There had been no camping during the long rainy season following the dome-building trip. The first camping trip of the dry season began on the Saturday after Christmas and ended on Tuesday January 2, 2120, the last day of winter break. Richard Russo led the group, but Stella declined to go along. "I love you," she told her new husband, "but I am not a camper. Sophie and I have some serious baking to do and I have those fingerling trout to look after. You can tell me all about your camping trip when you get home."

It was on this trip that a group of kudzu divers offered Michael several large pieces of aluminum roofing material. He had no use for articles that size and no way to get them home, but Richard said he would pay cash for the roofing material if the sellers would deliver it to the barn area. A deal was struck, the aluminum was delivered, and Richard started drawing up plans for a new building project.

Michael figured that he, Jesse, and Dylan would be asked to do the building. "I hope this is going to be something I'll need to know how to do when I get to Mars," Michael said to his friends.

Jesse shrugged his shoulders. "All experiences are useful, and any knowledge is good to have. You never know when it will come in handy."

Dylan spoke up. "You'll be doing your share, Jesse. Please remember that Michael and I worked on a huge building project last year while you spent the summer on maneuvers with your ROTC buddies." He gave his brother a dirty look. "Next time I'll crawl around in the dirt and play hide and seek while you work your fingers to the bone weaving kudzu."

Jesse refused to take the bait. He wasn't going to argue with somebody who had spent his volunteer hours making raincoats for a bunch of goats. He turned to Michael. "How about you?" he asked. "Do you think you worked harder last summer than I did?"

"No way," said Michael. "It was the easiest thing I ever did. I just kept my eyes on the girl of my dreams and the time flew by."

The discussion was over, but Dylan was determined that his brother would help to build whatever it was Uncle Richard had in mind, and if there was any kudzu weaving involved he would see that Jesse would be the one to do it.

chapter fourteen:
the documentary

"Do your best and leave the rest to God."

Japanese Proverb

embers of the graduating class faced the end of their winter break with a mixture of curiosity and dread. When other students went to their first period classes, the seniors gathered in the school auditorium to watch The Documentary. The Documentary had first been broadcast in 2090, the fiftieth anniversary of the great earthquakes and fires, and had been shown every January thereafter to all senior class members in South Carolina's public schools.

The Documentary had been produced by Furman students who pored over thousands of hours of video footage and conducted dozens of interviews. During the 2080s, earthquake survivors had been photographed before a green screen, quietly relating their experiences. Narration and background footage had been added and years of painstaking work had been edited into a six-hour program.

Hundreds of hours of unused interviews and historical footage were archived along with copies of the finished work at Furman University, the Smithsonian, and the Library of Congress. Viewing The Documentary was a rite of passage for

South Carolina's eighteen-year-olds, who watched it all on one day, with short breaks mid-morning and mid-afternoon and an hour for lunch.

Footage of upstate South Carolina before, during, and after the Brevard Fault quake accompanied the voice of an unseen announcer. An elderly woman appeared, walking before the giant screen to a chair placed front and center. She sat down and looked into the camera, old burn scars faintly visible through the make-up on her face and neck, and began to speak in a quiet voice.

"My name is Inez Masters. I went to work as an administrative assistant in Mayor Hope's office in 2034, right out of college. The Greenville area was a big manufacturing center, known for its automotive research center, car and bus makers, and parts manufacturers. The city and the county were quite prosperous. The Chamber of Commerce, County Planning Commission, and City of Greenville all had money to spend and wanted to spend it wisely.

"Disaster preparedness was on everybody's minds back then, just it is now. The County Planning Commission had drawn up several scenarios for the future of Greenville County. Most of these scenarios revolved around the expected growth of jobs and population. Some addressed problems caused by the continuing decline in air quality. There were detailed plans for community responses to terrorist attacks and natural disasters. Plans included emergency shelters in subterranean bunkers, emergency supplies hidden in mountain caves, even a small fusion plant tucked away in an abandoned quarry.

"We planned for the worst, but most of us thought the worst would never happen. I was at most of the meetings and I heard endless debates with people arguing and calling each other names. But in the end, we were ready, as ready as we could be, I guess. The weather kept getting worse. All across the country there were earthquakes, tornadoes, hurricanes and floods. After Yellowstone blew up, things got steadily worse. There were earthquakes in Tennessee and upper South Carolina, then we had one here."

Inez Masters paused for a moment, and then continued. "The ground shaking, buildings collapsing, and then the fires, it just seemed like the end of the world. But some of us made it. The younger, faster people made it into the shelters. Some of us had to race through flames to get there. They called it our "Katrina moment" when we all squeezed together in the bunkers. We had fire instead of water to deal with, and we were underground instead of underwater, but the feeling was the same, I guess. It really did feel like the end of the world, like Hades, like Armageddon, like your worst nightmare. But we survived."

The scene changed and a slender, well-dressed black man walked briskly across the stage. He sat down and looked into the camera.

"My name is Mitchell Stone," he said. "I was six years old when the first earthquake hit Rock Hill on New Year's Day 2040. My mother and I lived in Rock Hill but we had spent the holidays in Greenville with my grandparents. We were putting things in the car, getting ready to leave, when we felt the ground move slightly beneath our feet. I hardly even noticed it. Grandpa checked the news on his phone, then he told Mama and me that we needed to take our things back in the house."

He paused and wiped his eyes. "That was the first Rock Hill earthquake. Grandma took me into the kitchen and made me a peanut butter and jelly sandwich. She sat there and talked with me while I ate it. The rest of the grown-ups were in the other room, watching the news on TV. Grandma told me that Mama and I were not going to go back home just yet, that we would be staying with her and Grandpa awhile longer.

"Mama and I never did go home again. Our old lives were gone. There was nothing to go back to. She found a new job and I went to a new school. We hadn't completely adjusted to our new lives when the big earthquake hit Greenville on May 25. The grown-ups grabbed their suitcases and I put my favorite toys in a tote bag, and we headed for the nearest shelter.

"We lived underground for over a year. There were a lot of children there. There were school areas and play areas, all underground. Sometimes we pretended to be on a submarine, and drew pictures of fish and other things we thought we would see deep in the ocean. Mostly we pretended to be space travelers. We drew pictures of planets and stars and galaxies and put them on the walls where we thought a spaceship's windows would be, and pretended we were traveling across the universe faster than the speed of light."

The scene changed and another speaker was sitting on the chair as the slideshow continued in the background. "My name is Joseph Travis," he said. He seemed to have difficulty speaking, but formed his words carefully and took his time. "I was a young rookie policeman then. It was my job to guide people into the shelters. We kept count of how many went into each one. The shelters were rigid stainless steel containers buried in concrete. They were designed to withstand an earthquake, and the passageways connecting them were designed to maintain their integrity while flexing under pressure. In other words they were earthquake proof too, but in a different way. We filled the shelters to capacity and kept sending people in. Refugees were in storerooms, infirmaries, offices, and sitting on the floors of the passageways. We didn't turn anyone away.

"Some showed up empty-handed, some brought everything but the kitchen sink. We had to tell quite a few people to leave most of their possessions behind. A lot of them took it pretty hard, but we had our jobs to do. We told them to bring just the equivalent of carry-on luggage. They had to make some quick decisions, grab part of their stuff, and go inside. Some were pretty unhappy about it though. That's just human nature."

The tone of his voice changed slightly. "The hardest part was that so many people brought their pets. All the available shelter space had to go to humans, and animals had to be left behind.

Children were crying, adults cried too, but there was no choice. Humane Society volunteers were there, taking animals from their owners and putting them into cages. They said they would try to bring the pets in after all the people were inside. But the flames kept getting closer, the shelters were packed, and a few stragglers were still showing up. Finally the volunteers went around the cages with hypodermic needles and euthanized all the animals."

On the big screen were rows of cages with people moving hurriedly among them as the fire kept coming closer. His face expressionless, Joe Travis continued speaking.

"When the flames were almost upon us, I held the heavy door open while the Humane Society folks rushed through it. Then I stepped inside and pulled the door shut behind me. My own dog was in one of those cages. I never asked the volunteers if they were able to inject all of the animals before they threw their needles down and ran from the fire. I've always wanted to believe that they did. This is the first time I've told anybody about this.

"I was the very last person to enter the shelter. I stood at the top of the steps for a few minutes after everyone else disappeared into the tunnel, thinking about my dog. I placed my hand against the fireproof door and pulled it back in a hurry. That massive door was already too hot to touch."

The Announcer spoke again: "The shelters were stoutly built metal bunkers, designed to resist almost anything, including earthquakes. People with serious injuries were moved into a hospital under the heart of Piney Mountain, and cared for until they no longer needed care. Babies born there were moved into the infirmary until mothers felt ready to return with them to the shelters."

The scene changed and another man appeared before the giant screen. "My name is Ronald Terence," he said. "I was a firefighter. We weren't able to put out all the fires, but we did what we could and we helped people get to safety, and at the last minute we squeezed in with them. Later, when the fires had died down, we came up from the shelters. A number of volunteers came with us, all of us wearing boots and masks and heavy gloves. We waded through the warm ashes and set to work clearing several acres of ground. We put twisted metal and other salvaged items on sledges and hauled them to an area where the debris could be sorted and stored. Soon there were so many stacks of bricks and piles of debris that more ground had to be cleared just to hold all the salvaged materials. Other volunteers sorted the debris while we kept bringing more. Sometimes there were burnt vehicles and other debris too large to move so we left them in place and worked around them. We could see smoke in the distance and we worked carefully to make sure there were no lingering embers that might flare up around us.

"The whole job took several days. We raked the ashes evenly across the cleared land, watered the place down good, and set up enough tents to hold three thousand men. I was young and single, so I was one of them. It wasn't a bad place to live. Several large tents were designated for use as mess halls or restrooms. Oxygen concentrators were installed in all of the tents. Fortunately for us, the rainy season held off until everything was in place."

The Announcer's voice was heard again: "When the rain came, bringing winds that shook the tents and threatened to blow them from their moorings, some men cursed the tent city, wishing they were still underground where, no matter how cramped conditions were, at least they were dry.

"Many tent dwellers were teachers and other skilled workers who returned daily to the bunkers to work in makeshift schools, help with never-ending preparation and distribution of food, and perform other necessary services in the refugee community. The rest of the men were deputized and worked alongside professional security officers to guard the tent city and the shelter entrances. The daily lives of the shelter dwellers fell into a rhythm that resembled normal life, but life in the outside world continued to be chaotic and dangerous. The desperation and lawlessness of that period led to the forming of a society almost feudal in nature."

The scene changed and a woman sat before the screen,

hesitating for a moment before she began: "My name is Lucia Becker. I was a middle school teacher and I was in my classroom when the earthquake hit. Our principal sent alerts to the parents and then we took our students to safety, according to a pre-arranged plan that all of the parents had signed off on. Most of the children were eventually reunited with their families. Some families survived intact, some did not, and many of our students never saw any of their family members again.

"In the bunkers, groups formed small neighborhoods with play areas for the children. We set up classrooms with whatever school supplies were available. My students and I had brought everything we could carry, and others had done the same. There were also some textbooks and other things in a storeroom under the mountain, so we managed quite well. We had a pretty good school system up and running in less than a week, and we kept our children busy the whole time I was there.

"People put their skills to use where they could do the most good. They prepared and distributed food, cared for the sick and injured, and formed committees to address every possible need. The oldest members of the community devoted themselves to the sick and injured, providing companionship and assistance where it was needed, and helping to care for the children in the convalescent center. A strong feeling of fellowship developed throughout the group."

She hesitated, and then resumed speaking. "My husband was at work in his downtown office when the earthquake struck. He never had a chance. Our four-month-old baby was brought to the shelter by his day care workers. They got all of their charges to safety, texing the parents while they were bringing our children to the shelters so we would know they were all right. One of them brought little Philip to me on our second day there. All we had were the contents of his diaper bag and my purse. We couldn't have gotten through that awful time without the help of the wonderful people around us. A few months later, I turned my classroom over to someone else and returned to North Carolina. We moved in with my parents and I found a job in the Mecklenburg County school system."

After a fifteen-minute break in mid-morning, the interviews continued. A doctor spoke about giving everyone potassium iodide for protection against radioactivity from the damaged nuclear plant. Two people told of becoming orphans and being cared for by volunteers.

Then another man sat before the screen and spoke to the camera. "My name is Will Snyder. I was the chief engineer in the Greenville County Public Works Department. The surviving city and county employees held weekly meetings to decide what we should do next. The small nuclear fusion plant in the old quarry had come through like a champ, providing electric power beyond our needs, and the mountain storehouse had held enough computers to bring the city and county government back on line. Once all of the back-up files were retrieved from satellite storage and reinstalled on the stored equipment, it was almost business as usual. Things could have been much worse.

"We installed interactive video screens in all of the bunkers and security cameras in every tunnel. Some folks complained about Big Brother watching them, but most people considered the idea more of a comfort than a threat, at least in their current circumstances. They had survived the worst, and they would be grateful for any improvement in their present condition. We were able to keep everyone informed and to have town meetings and referendums. The whole idea actually worked pretty well."

Finally it was time for lunch. "Not a moment too soon," grumbled Sophie. "I'm not sure I can eat anything, but I'm ready for a break anyway. This is just too much. Now I know why we had to wait until we were eighteen to see The Documentary, and I hope we never have to look at it again."

"That's because your family wasn't living here then," said Sharon. "My mother's family was in North Carolina, but I'm pretty sure my Dad's folks lived around here someplace. I know he lived here in the 90s. I'm going to ask him about it."

"I actually saw my grandfather on the screen," said Deeya. "He never mentioned being in a documentary. He never talked about that time in his life at all. He told me he was from Rock Hill but grew up in Greenville, but he never talked about any of this."

"I guess he had his reasons," commented Megan. "People don't like to discuss that sort of thing, especially with children. Not much has been said at my house, although I know my grandfather was a child when it happened. He wasn't in the documentary but his older brother was. He was the one who lost his dog. He met and married his wife in the shelters. They were in the group that moved into the second dome, so they lived in one of the bunkers for the first few years of their marriage."

Megan's friends stared at her, surprised by her words.

"I know," she said. "Not the best place for a honeymoon, but older people and families with children got preference for the first dome, and after they moved out, many of the bunkers were divided into apartments. The rest of the people lived there until another dome was built."

The girls finished their lunch and found other things to talk about until it was time to return to the auditorium.

The Documentary focused now on the problems of a new society and the reasoning behind moving into habitat domes. "The situation was an insurance adjustor's nightmare," said the Announcer. "It would take years to resolve all the property issues. Many insurance companies had folded. If an insurance company were still in business, the settlements would be pennies on the dollar. However, there was none of that just then. Something had to be done as quickly and cheaply as possible to find new homes for everyone. City and county officials tried vainly to negotiate a consensus among the electorate. Finally Mayor Hope announced that he had made an executive decision with which the County Commission was in perfect agreement. A glass habitat dome would be erected and brick apartment buildings would be built inside it. All law-abiding county residents will be eligible to live there. "

The Announcer was silent as Mayor Hope's face appeared on the big screen, giving the speech that had been watched on video screens throughout the shelters and tents.

"It will be a long time before the quality of our air is restored," the Mayor declared. "It will barely support life now. Even our soil is tainted. Children need clean air and clean food to help their brains and bodies develop properly. For now, living under a sealed dome is the healthiest and safest choice for families with children, and is already a way of life in many communities. We offer this option to all of our current residents. No monetary payment will be required, but residents must agree to work for the community in return for the shelter and services they receive."

The Mayor smiled. "We'll continue to live as we do now, but in a more desirable environment. Some of our local manufacturing plants have resumed operation, and cash is beginning to flow into the community once more. The county has arranged for loans to cover the cost of dome construction, and as local industries ramp up production, there will be money from taxes to repay that debt. We are certain this plan will work, but anyone who doesn't wish to participate is free to leave at any time. When the dome is ready for occupancy, the tent city will come down and the shelters will close."

The Announcer spoke again. "The refugee population had been constantly changing. Families left to join relatives elsewhere, young adults enlisted in the armed forces, veterans re-enlisted, and many engineers and skilled workers left for contract positions elsewhere, leaving their families behind.

"As shelter dwellers left, they were replaced by people from smaller public and private shelters in the area. The County Commission pledged to erect a large dome where it would be possible to live for six months on a trial basis before signing a long-term contract. Using borrowed and donated money and equipment, construction of the dome began."

The dome's steel frame was erected by experienced dome-builders from the Pittsburgh area. Time lapse photography showed huge steel beams swinging from giant cranes as the frame was assembled. Work stopped when the dry season ended, and resumed months later when the sun came out again. When the framing was finished, a topping out ceremony was held and onlookers cheered as an American flag was raised on top of the steel skeleton.

Starting from the top and circling downward around the skeletal structure, workers immediately began installing and sealing huge panes of glass. After one-third of the glass had been installed, the rains began again. Three months later, the rain ended and work was resumed, and before it returned, the job was finished and the dome was sealed.

Rainy seasons were no deterrent to the next phase of the project. A basement was dug and filled with a complicated maze of tunnels, pipes, and utility rooms. Sticking up among them were the footings for a dozen large apartment buildings and other structures. A basement ceiling/dome floor of reinforced concrete was laid over the basement, with the brick footings rising slightly above it. At the same time, bricks salvaged from the kudzu were cleaned and stacked in a nearby clearing. After the floor had cured, the bricks were brought into the dome and construction on the buildings began.

The Documentary ended as the first group of dome dwellers carried their belongings into their new apartments and closed the doors behind them.

At last Documentary Day was over. It had been overwhelming. The students understood why they hadn't seen it before. Some wondered why they had been required to see it at all. Few would ever watch it again.

No homework was assigned to the seniors that afternoon,

which was a good thing, as during each break several students had slipped away and did not return to school until the following day.

That evening, the Travis twins were unusually quiet at the supper table.

"What's the matter? Has the cat got your tongue?" their father asked them.

Mary looked at her husband. "They saw The Documentary today, John. They have a lot on their minds right now."

"I'm sorry, kids," John told his children. "I forgot what day this was."

"There is a reason why visuals and audios are never downloaded into data chips," said Mary. "Nobody wants something like that so close to their brain. I believe everyone should see The Documentary at least once, but you shouldn't have to download it and carry it around with you all the time."

"That's true," said Megan. "There wasn't much we didn't already know, but seeing it up there on the big screen really brought it home."

"The musical score reminded me of the old Lucas and Spielberg movies you watch," said Michael.

"I don't recall seeing any aliens in The Documentary," commented John. "Did they put some in since I saw it in 2090?"

Megan smiled. "We're not telling," she said. "Watch it yourself if you're curious enough. But let me ask you something. Your Uncle Joe was in it. Whatever happened to him?"

Colonel Travis cleared his throat, a sure sign that he was going to say something significant. He paused, and then spoke very carefully.

"Uncle Joe and Aunt Emily were in no hurry to start a family. They wanted to get settled in a dome and established in their careers first. In 2049, Uncle Joe was up for a promotion and had a thorough physical exam. That's when he learned he carried a gene for Huntington's disease. He and Aunt Emily decided not to have any children. He developed the illness when he was in his fifties, and was still in the early stages when he was interviewed in 2084. By the time The Documentary was shown in 2090, he had become totally bedridden. He passed away a few years later.

"My mother was pregnant with me when Uncle Joe learned about the Huntington's gene and my father got tested right away. They were devastated to learn that he and I both had the gene. I received stem cell treatments in utero, and was considered cured, but I've never been convinced that it's completely out of my system and I never wanted to risk passing it along. Dad and Uncle Joe got stem cell treatments too, but back then the treatment was not very effective in adults. Dad was able to work until he was in his sixties, but he passed away shortly after he retired."

Michael was taken by surprise. "Why haven't you told us this before?"

Mary answered that one. "You didn't ask," she said simply. "And besides it was irrelevant because neither you nor your sister has the gene."

"Mom, is that why you and Dad never had a baby? Because of that one gene?" asked Megan.

"We just decided it was better not to take any chances. Besides, we wanted to serve together in the military, and knew we couldn't take children everywhere we went. We enlisted as a couple, served our country, and saw the world together, parts of it anyway. Then we retired after twenty years of service and came home. We believed if we were meant to have a family, the opportunity would present itself. Which it did, and we're happy with the way things turned out."

"Amazing," said Michael. "Mom, Dad, I hope I haven't let you down. Sorry about that moving to Mars thing."

"So am I, Son, a little bit," said John. "But you haven't let me down. I know you have to follow your own path just as I followed mine. Besides, once you get settled in, your Mom and I just might come to Mars for a visit, or at least meet you at Disney Moon for a nice vacation."

"May I come too, Dad?" asked Megan. "The farthest I've ever been from home is that dome-weaving trip to Gaffney."

They all started laughing, imagining the grown-up Megan taken to Disney Moon by her doting parents. The whole idea of having a family reunion at Disney Moon was funny anyway. When the laughter died down, Mary remembered an ad she had seen recently, touting the advantages of living in one of the Moon's new retirement communities. She decided to tex the company to request more information.

chapter fifteen: visions

"You can steer yourself any direction you choose."

from "Oh, the Places You'll Go!"
by Theodor Seuss Geisel

Time spent on Richard Russo's projects counted toward volunteer hours, and the work was usually interesting. Dylan and Michael enjoyed herding goats in dry weather, and the building projects could be fun. The latest project, building a new home for the rapidly growing trout, was a little more complicated than most.

To begin with, four nanny goats, too old for breeding or milking, were brought outside to clear a strip of land adjacent to the barns. Bewildered, the nannies huddled next to the kudzu. They were indoor goats, elderly and unaccustomed to being outdoors.

Dylan plucked some young leaves and offered them to the nannies. Recognizing their favorite food, they began munching on the tender leaves. He then stepped into the kudzu thicket and demonstrated what he wanted "the ladies" to do.

When Michael saw Dylan gnawing vines and chewing leaves, he burst into laughter and shot some choice footage with his phone, but he had to admit that Dylan's plan worked. The goats got the idea and burrowed into the thicket where they quickly began stripping leaves from the thickest vines and devouring the smaller vines completely.

Dylan and Michael followed the goats, severing the stripped vines about a foot above the ground and cutting them into twelve-foot sections. The clearing grew as old animals and young men worked together in the winter sun. As they had done at the tannery, the boys laid cut vines on large nets and prepared them to be hoisted and carried to the drying barn by the same minicraft used to haul vines from the tannery. The mini didn't have to make many trips; the goats were doing a pretty thorough job of clearing the kudzu.

Working at ground level to fasten a kudzu-filled net to the mini's skids was a bit trickier than it had been on the tannery platform, but they got it done. The big problem was every time the mini hovered over the clearing, the goats went into a panic, bleating and pulling at their tethers. Michael got some footage of that too. After the first day in the clearing, the elderly nannies alternated with two teams of rowdy young billies, clearing away kudzu while Michael and Dylan were in school. The boys came to the clearing every afternoon to bundle kudzu and gather goat droppings. Soon the new clearing was ready for the next stage of the project, in which they were not involved.

It was several weeks before Michael and Dylan returned to the clearing, bringing Jesse with them. The huge kudzu roots had been dug up and taken to the processing plant and the site had been graded. Down the center of the long narrow clearing was a pit three feet deep, fifteen feet wide, and sixty feet long. A six-inch layer of concrete had been poured into the trench to form the bottom of the fish tanks. The concrete had cured and now the young volunteers were going to learn something about bricklaying.

Michael, Dylan, and Jesse worked as hod carriers for brick masons who built the sides of the new fish tanks and did whatever else needed doing at the site while the masons, flashing their trowels, put the bricks into place with swift precision. After the sides rose above ground level, the boys were allowed to do some closely supervised bricklaying of their own until the fish tanks stood four feet above the ground. The long sides of the tank were then lined with a row of sturdy brick columns, one row a foot taller than the other, which the boys helped to build. When it was time to transform each line of columns into a row of classic brick arches, two master masons took over while other bricklayers watched and learned.

"Too bad there was no kudzu-weaving on this project," Jesse said to his brother. "I was really looking forward to it."

"I'm sure you were," said Dylan. "I'm sorry you were disappointed. Better luck next time."

Jesse and Amy spent the following weekend on maneuvers with their ROTC unit, Michael hopped a shuttle to Charlotte to visit Luna, and Dylan helped his mother with a couple of catering jobs.

Susan Murray was Special Events Manager for Francesca's Kitchen, and often pressed Dylan into service as a singing waiter. That weekend he served and sang at a wedding reception and an anniversary party, collecting tips from the honorees. His cousin Sophie worked as a server at both events, and on Saturday afternoon she dressed as a princess to serve cake and ice cream at a birthday party for Mayor Cresitello's daughter.

The fishery's aluminum roof was added later by professional roofers who quickly fashioned a sturdy kudzu web to support a flat aluminum roof that extended slightly past the lower side of the tank. The roofers shaped the overhanging metal into a channel directing rainwater into a large cistern. Then the tanks were filled with purified water and the trout were introduced to their new home.

Spring break came and went. Michael spent most of it in Charlotte, staying at the Becker home under the close supervision of Luna's grandparents. He and Luna went out and about together, even visiting the Gastonia complex where they spent half an hour browsing in a shop called Wanda's Treasure Chest. They found Sharon working there, taking inventory and stocking shelves.

"This place belongs to my Aunt Wanda," Sharon told them. She introduced them to her aunt, who promptly put an Out for Lunch sign in the window and took the three young people to a nearby café for soup and sandwiches.

Soon it was time for the Senior Prom. Dylan told Megan that none of his former girlfriends would accept his invitation, and that the kudzu-grazing pictures of him that her brother had pasted on YouTube would prevent him from ever finding a date for anything.

"What about Julianna and what's-her-name from last summer?" Megan wanted to know.

"It's too expensive to bring one of them down for the weekend and I can't invite a girl and then tell her she has to pay her own way," he answered. "Besides they've seen the goat pictures too. That stuff Michael posted on YouTube went viral. You know that. To make matters worse, he included some of the old goat raincoat footage along with it. Some friend he is! He didn't realize how bad it would be for me, and he did apologize, but just the same he has totally ruined my social life."

"I guess you'll die a lonely bachelor," said Megan, "or maybe when you're in your forties you'll get married to somebody you've just met, like your Uncle Richard."

"I should be so lucky," said Dylan. "So what are you going to do? Two guys in the drum corps have told me they asked you to Prom and you turned them both down. Do you have a date or not?"

"I thought you'd never ask," said Megan. "I feel it's my responsibility to go to the Prom with you since it was my brother who single-handedly ruined your social life. Be warned that I'll expect to do a lot of dancing since I'm not in charge of anything this time."

"What color corsage do you want?" asked Dylan.

"White would go with anything I might decide to wear," said Megan. "And I'll get you a white boutonniere."

Another rainy season was well under way when the Senior Prom was held in early May. Trader Bill and his wife "Miss Annie," who would be photographer/chaperones, flew down for the occasion, bringing Alec and his friend Will, who were on a weekend pass from their military school.

Luna came with them and went to the Prom with Michael. Will escorted Sharon, Alec escorted Deeya, and Sophie brought Max, a Furman student and part-time Francesca's Kitchen employee. As agreed, Dylan and Megan went to the prom together.

The Prom's theme was "Visions of the Future," which seemed quite suitable for the about-to-be graduates. Michael and Luna slipped out for awhile to have some quiet time together, returning to the dance floor in time for the coronation ceremonies. To their great surprise, Michael was crowned King and Megan was chosen to be a Lady of the Court. Young people danced the night away as chaperones dozed in their chairs. The next day, the out-of-towners hurried through the rain to Trader Bill's hovercraft, and headed north with Alec at the controls.

Soon the school year ended. Commencement ceremonies in Greenville and Charlotte were held on the same weekend. Michael and Luna, unable to attend each other's graduations, swapped HoloCam footage and congratulated each other in virtual fashion, as both of them were honor graduates. In addition, Michael received an award for public service and Luna was voted Most Likely to Succeed.

In Greenville, Trader Bill and Miss Annie beamed with pride when Sharon was honored as valedictorian. "I guess that data chip paid off," Annie whispered to her husband, who was too busy with his HoloCam to respond. Dylan was recognized for his musical talents, Deeya was recognized for her creativity, and Megan was shocked to learn she had been voted Most Likely to Succeed.

Michael applauded loudly when Megan accepted her award. Unknown to his sister, he had done a lot of politicking to swing the votes her way. Megan had a way of pulling people together to get things done, while staying in the background and letting others get most of the credit. Michael had quietly reminded his classmates of her accomplishments, and his efforts had paid off.

The following weekend, the Sullivan family flew to Virginia for Alec's graduation ceremonies. He looked striking in his uniform, and accepted his diploma with dignity. After the ceremony the Sullivan family went out to dinner with Alec's friend Will and his parents. Listening to Will and Alec talk about their undergraduate escapades, the young men's parents heaved a collective sigh of relief that their sons had made it through military school without spending time in the brig.

Will had been accepted into the Military Academy, but Alec was ready to shuck his uniform and help his father with the family business. "I'm going to join the National Guard instead," he declared. "I want to study online for a business degree and see if we can't ramp up the family firm a bit, see how big we can make it grow."

Miss Annie rolled her eyes at her husband, who responded with a genial wink. "We'll talk about that later," he said to Alec.

Luna and Michael were together a lot that summer, parting reluctantly to go their separate ways. Michael entered the Space Academy and Luna enrolled at Furman to complete the dual degrees in chemistry and biology toward which she been accumulating credits throughout high school.

Luna decided to be a day student, staying in Greenville with the Travis family. She grew very close to Mary, a no-nonsense woman with a lot of insight into the human condition, and formed a sisterly bond with Megan, but was always a bit in awe of John Travis, a dignified man referred to by his children as the Colonel. During her years in his household, Luna always addressed him as "Sir."

Dylan, Deeya, and Megan chose Furman also, Dylan as a music major, Deeya with an art scholarship, and Megan majoring in chemistry and biology with an eye on medical school.

Sophie enrolled in a culinary program at Greenville Tech. Steve Lin was not all happy about his daughter's choice. "Sophie could teach that stuff," he told his wife. "She ought to be getting a business degree so she can run this place someday."

"Maybe she'll marry an accountant like I did," said Patricia. "Cooking is a lot more fun."

Jesse and Amy left together for the Military Academy, Sharon headed north to major in political science at Rutgers, and Alec began working for Trader Bill's Treasures, studying online for a business degree and dreaming of the day when he could grow the family firm into a global corporation.

chapter sixteen: trader bill

"May the road rise up to meet you...
May good friends be there to greet you"

from an old Irish blessing

William Sullivan, aka Trader Bill, had grown up in the Greenville dome and graduated from Greenville High School in 2098. Gregarious and easy-going, he was a fair athlete, a decent student, a talented singer, and a good dancer. Early in December of their senior year, his friend Dan Hayes had come to him and said, "Trader, I need you to do me a favor."

Bill had acquired this nickname in the seventh grade, when he had begun coming to school with cookies saved from yesterday's dinner, a rusty pocketknife, a pair of socks he had outgrown, or anything else that he was hoping somebody would want. He was always ready to barter. If he had no need for what he received in trade, he would keep on swapping, trading up each time, until he was satisfied. He had recently turned eighteen, old enough to apply for a kudzu diving license, and had submitted his application that very day.

"Just what kind of a favor do you need?" Bill asked.

Dan explained the situation. "My next-door neighbors had

company Thanksgiving weekend, their son and his wife and two daughters. I met one of the girls and we've been texing ever since. I asked Wanda – that's her name - to be my date for the Winter Prom and she said not unless I get a date for her sister."

"You want me to go to the dance with some girl I've never met?"

"It's an ancient custom known as a blind date, Trader. Besides, you told me you didn't have a date for the dance."

"I don't have any money for a date," said Bill, "How would I pay for a corsage and something at the Smoothie Bar after? Besides, if I go alone, I can dance with anybody I want to. What if I'm stuck all night with a girl who has two left feet and I can't get anybody else to take her off my hands?"

Dan pulled out his phone. "Here's Wanda's picture," he said. "She and Annie are identical twins. I'll lend you the money for the corsage and stuff and you can pay me back when you sell whatever junk you find on your first dive."

Bill looked at the picture. "Did you say identical twins?" he asked.

"Identical," said Dan.

Bill took another look. "Done," he said. "Give me her number and I'll do the rest."

Exactly one month later, Bill walked up to Dan and said, "I sold everything I brought up on my first dive. Here's your money with 100% interest to thank you for introducing me to my future wife."

More than twenty-five years after his first and last blind date, Bill Sullivan was still known as Trader Bill and still intrigued by the mysteries lying beneath the kudzu, although he no longer suited up and dove through the tangled thickets in search of hidden treasure.

A company called Mega Salvage was the biggest kudzu-diving organization in North America. Mega Salvage did a big business retrieving and selling useful materials found in the kudzu-covered ruins of twenty-first century civilization. There was a great demand for scrap metal and usable wood. Almost anything brought up from the depths of the kudzu could be put to use in some way. Their well-equipped divers were prepared to handle almost any kind of large-scale salvage operation.

Mega Salvage's contracts with Mega Metals and Mega Construction gave those companies exclusive rights to purchase all scrap metal, bricks, unbroken glass panes (rare and extremely valuable), and other usable construction materials that Mega Salvage divers found among the ruins.

Many small companies vied for the opportunity to purchase other items, and were eager to sign contracts for the privilege. One successful bidder was Trader Bill's Treasures, owned by Bill and his wife Anne, known to their customers as "Miss Annie."

Trader Bill was a discerning picker, specializing in small items such as flash drives, memory cards, plastic and ceramic tableware, kitchenware, and decorative items. He knew the needs and preferences of his regular customers, and when restocking his hovercraft at Mega Salvage warehouses, kept an eye out for things they would appreciate. He also was an agent for his wife's sister Wanda, who owned a small home accessories shop under the dome of the Gastonia Mall. Bill loved to tease his sister-in-law, joking that she bought old junk and sold rare antiques. He could just as well have said that she bought rare antiques and sold old junk, as the items he chose on her behalf were always valued for their rarity and elegance despite being the worse for wear after spending years beneath the kudzu. "Wanda's Treasure Chest" was a favorite destination for serious shoppers from miles around, and her blog was a must-read for them as well.

Anne and Wanda maintained an on-line catalog with pictures of especially valuable or unusual acquisitions, selling most of them through on-line auctions and the rest on consignment in Wanda's store. Trader Bill also delivered the on-line purchases while making his rounds. The three of them had a nice little family business.

One rainy January day in 2123, Trader Bill landed his craft on the mud near Greenville's Administration Dome to keep an appointment with Deeya Stone, an intern in the Habitat Planning Department.

Totally enveloped in a large hooded cape, under which he clasped a bulky package close to his chest, Trader Bill slogged through the thick red mud to reach the Dome's entrance. The security guards welcomed him, one of them taking his package as another guard helped him remove his raingear and mask.

"Trader, you must be bringing something pretty special for you to deliver it in this weather," one of the guards commented.

"We'll know just how special it is after Miss Deeya sees it," replied Trader Bill.

Half an hour later, Dan Hayes, Chairman of the Greenville Planning Commission, Deeya Stone, and several county and city employees stood around a table as Trader Bill began to speak.

"On January 1, 2040, a major earthquake hit the Rock Hill area, followed by fires that burned for several weeks. The ruins were abandoned as survivors moved elsewhere, and much of the area was unstable for years. Mega's divers recently started working there, and until yesterday they hadn't turned up much except scrap metal and blackened bricks."

Trader Bill paused and laid his carefully wrapped package on the conference table. "Yesterday my wife got an urgent tex from one of the crew leaders. His divers had brought up several safes from the old Carolina Film Studios. When the safes were opened, one was found to contain a number of very interesting books. Everyone knows that Miss Annie has accumulated a magnificent collection of mildewed, worm-eaten, and half-burnt books over the years, and the message suggested that she ought to come over right away and take a look."

"Here, Deeya," he said, smiling at the puzzled young woman. "You do the honors."

Deeya knew Trader Bill very well. His daughter Sharon

had lived with Deeya's family while she attended high school in Greenville, and the girls were close friends.

Deeya began carefully unwrapping what she soon realized was a large book. It proved to be a sketchbook, fragile but intact. She looked questioningly at Trader. "Open it and see what you think," he told her.

Deeya lifted the sketchbook from its wrappings and held it carefully, opening the cover to read the inscription inside. "It says 'Property of Lydia Jones.' This is unbelievable!" she exclaimed. "Lydia Jones was my great-grandmother."

Tears filled the young woman's eyes. "I've always known the story. My grandfather was a child when the big earthquake struck Rock Hill. His mother was the head designer for Carolina Film Studios. She designed sets and clothing for all their movies. They were down here visiting her parents when it happened, and they never went back home. There was nothing left to go back to."

She paused and wiped her eyes. "There were earthquakes in other parts of the state later that year, even here in Greenville County. Everything changed after that, not just for them but for everyone."

There was silence in the room. It was common knowledge that the twenty-first century had been a time of Apocalyptic events, but this was never discussed. Not until today, by a young woman overcome with surprise and emotion.

"Deeya, our friends at Mega Salvage want you to have this book. It's yours to keep. But they found a lot more, and that's another reason why I'm here today." Trader pulled out his HoloCam and removed the holostick, handing it to Dan Hayes. "The divers found a cedar-lined vault filled with period clothing, bolts of cloth, and other valuable items you might be interested in for the new Arts Center you're planning. Mega will be accepting bids for all of these things as soon as the inventory is completed. Here are the pictures I took. You wouldn't believe the quality of those fabrics after so many years in storage."

"I can't thank you enough for bringing us the inside scoop," said Chairman Hayes. "This is a lot to think about."

"Time is of the essence," Trader replied. "I don't know what kind of budget you're working with, but you need to send someone up there to take a look, and the sooner the better. Everything is in Mega's York County warehouse, at least for now, but it might be moved to Charlotte soon for public display. Some of those things belong in a museum."

"Probably everything should be in a museum, but it would be tempting to buy some of the costumes for the Arts Center, if we could afford them. And the fabrics must be priceless." Dan Hayes took his phone from its case and began texing rapidly. "We'll have a meeting tonight to go through your pictures and talk things over, and I'll send you a note afterward."

Hugging the sketchbook, Deeya looked up at Trader. "Uncle Bill, are you sure I can keep this book? It must be priceless too."

"Deeya, my dear," said Trader, "I am certain. Just remember you may be asked to lend it out from time to time. It's great source material for historians and would ordinarily be in a museum. But it belongs to you, and here is the document to prove it." He handed her a sealed envelope.

"Now I have to go. The weather isn't good today, and I'd like to get back before dark."

Trader Bill shook hands with his old friend Dan, nodded at the rest of the group gathered around the table, and left. Soon he was at the controls of his hovercraft, singing a lusty rendition of "Yellow Submarine" as he headed home through the pouring rain.

chapter seventeen:
at the end of the rainbow

"There's a kiss at the end of the rainbow,
more precious than a pot of gold."

from "A Kiss At The End Of The Rainbow"
by McKean and O'Toole

On Christmas morning, 2122, Michael knelt before Luna and presented her with a ring she had admired on a recent visit to Wanda's Treasure chest, set with a heart-shaped diamond surrounded by emerald chips. "It's time to set a date for our wedding," he said, "and this makes it official."

Luna beamed with pleasure. "I knew the first time I saw you --"

Michael quickly interrupted her with a lingering kiss. "I knew before you did," he said afterward. "I actually knew even before I had a chance to see how beautiful you are. But at first you thought I was just a stalker, remember?"

She blushed. "Maybe so," she admitted. "But when I found out you were Megan's brother, I figured you had to be all right. And I really was a bit flattered by the attention."

On January 27, the first day of the Chinese Year of the Goat, Dylan proposed to Megan. She smiled and told him she would think it over. "Please don't mention this to anyone for now," she said. "If you don't change your mind, ask me again in June, after Michael and Luna have tied the knot."

"I guess that's a maybe," he answered.

Megan smiled. "Maybe it is," she said. "It's a tempting subject and clever of you to bring it up on this particular day, but it needs to be put on the back burner for awhile."

Dylan kissed her and then stepped back, shaking his head. "I will never understand women," he said. "You most of all."

"That's the way it should be," she replied. "Now I have a shower and a bachelorette party to plan and you need to start thinking about a bachelor party for my brother."

Preparations for a June wedding had already begun. Uncle Phil had bought a bundle of antique white satin from Mega Salvage, Luna's parents had booked a very special venue, Francesca's Kitchen had begun planning an off-site catering job, and Deeya had gotten measurements from all the females in the wedding party.

Megan, bemused but not entirely surprised by Dylan's proposal, had already been thinking about marriage to her brother's best friend. She knew Dylan's good qualities. He was talented, loyal, sincere, kind, a wonderful sweetheart and companion. "I believe we could have a good marriage," she thought, "even if I have to raise him along with our children." She knew she would eventually say yes, but not yet, not when announcing their engagement might draw attention away from the wedding of Michael and Luna. For now, everything had to be about her brother and his bride. They must have a perfect wedding that would create precious memories for them to cherish together on a distant world.

Luna's Great-Aunt Marilyn and Cousin Phyllis, experienced wedding planners, were putting it all together. Marilyn was actually Luna's Great-Great-Aunt but that was too much of a mouthful and besides she said it made her seem too old. Phyllis was Marilyn's daughter, which made her either Luna's third cousin or first cousin twice removed. Luna was never quite sure which. The wedding arrangements were safe in their capable hands.

During the next few months, Luna concentrated on her studies. She had completed BS degrees in Chemistry and Biology, passed all courses required for an MS in Horticultural Science, and begun writing a thesis on the medicinal properties of plants. She had been accepted by the Space Academy for a Preparation for Mars program running concurrently with her future husband's final year at the Academy. Finally, Luna and Michael would be living together and attending the same school.

At the end of April, Luna packed her belongings, said goodbye to her hosts, giving Mary Travis a grateful hug, and returned to Charlotte. She had completed and submitted her thesis and would return in a few weeks to defend it, after which she expected to download her diploma from the Furman website. In May, after wedding showers in Charlotte and Greenville, she was whisked away by Megan to a bachelorette party at a high-end spa in Gastonia, where she and all of her bridesmaids spent an entire day being pampered and beautified.

"This is really great!" exclaimed Luna. Holding a glass of wine in one hand and a kudzu crisp in the other, she raised her feet to admire her newly painted toenails. "My first pedicure! I didn't realize it could be so much fun!"

"I've never had one before either," said Megan. "Or a hot stone massage or a facial. I'm glad you like it. I think we're all enjoying your party." It was the first spa experience for everyone, and all of the young women declared it to be the highlight of the pre-wedding festivities.

After Michael's academic year ended, he and Luna spent Memorial Day weekend at their favorite bed and breakfast in Gaffney, finalizing arrangements for their June 12 wedding. The new habitat dome's crystals had matured, the subterranean tunnels and utilities were functioning smoothly, the buildings were ready for use, and the first dining hall was open. The managers of Morrison Foods, holder of the Gaffney franchise, were more than willing to help Francesca's Kitchen make the Reyes-Travis wedding an unforgettable event. The dome's interior surface was being coated with Solar Screen, a laborious process that must be finished before the new residents moved in. The work was nearly done, but coating the dome's apex would not be completed until after the wedding.

Dylan had heard all about the spa party, and wanted to arrange something equally memorable for Michael. "Do you have any suggestions?" he asked his Uncle Richard.

"I didn't have a bachelor party," said Richard. "I barely had a wedding. I've never even been to a bachelor party. Do you want to go out in the kudzu, hunt for wild boars and do manly things? Or get dressed up and go out on the town?"

"Something in between, I guess," answered Dylan. "Manly but not muddy, dressed up but not too wild, and no dancing girls or I'll never hear the end of it from Megan."

"I know someone who may be able to help us," said Richard. "I'll call him and get back to you."

On the day of the bachelor party, Alec and Will landed at the Greenville airstrip in Alec's new midicraft. They picked up Richard, Dylan, Jesse, Michael, and a few other friends, and headed for Doug Lawrence's home in a private community. The Lawrence family had recently left to spend the summer in the Adirondacks of upstate New York, and Doug had graciously offered Richard and his nephews the use of his home for the party.

They parked at the dome community's airstrip and showed their IDs to the security guards as they went inside, carrying hampers of food and wine for a memorable dinner.

"Quite a change from wild game cooked over a campfire," Jesse said afterward. "I could get used to this. Sophie really outdid herself."

Besides being the most elegant dwelling Michael had ever seen, the Lawrence home held a huge game room complete with billiard table, hologames, climbing wall, and antigravity sports chamber. Following Doug's texted instructions, Richard opened a cabinet and took out a humidor of Cuban cigars. "Smoke 'em if you dare," he told the younger men. "And don't mention this to anybody."

The party was every bit as memorable as Luna's spa day. "I'll certainly remember this when I'm a pioneer on Mars," Michael told his friends, waving their cigar smoke away from his face.

"Now you know how the other half lives," said Richard.

"Thank you for making this happen, Uncle Richard," Dylan told him. "We're all grateful to you and we're especially grateful to Mr. Lawrence and his family."

Soon the big day arrived. Rows of folding chairs faced a flower-bedecked altar. Uncle Phil, Uncle Richard, Jesse, and Alec ushered guests to their seats. The Gaffney Chamber Orchestra softly played the classical equivalent of elevator music as Reverend Gilder in his robe, Michael in his NASA uniform, and Dylan in his father's tuxedo took their places beneath the apex of the dome.

The music changed to Wagner's "Bridal Chorus" as the bridesmaids appeared. Megan, maid of honor, Abby, Amy, Deeya, Ellie, Sharon, Sophie, and Susie came down the aisle in knee-length white satin sheath dresses followed by Phyllis's granddaughter Lara, who wore a full-skirted white satin dress with a pink ribbon belt and pink ribbons in her hair. Lara carried a basket of pink and white rose petals which she sprinkled about in her most ladylike manner.

The bride made her appearance, ethereal in a long white satin gown and a crown of white roses, holding a white rose bouquet. Luna moved slowly down the aisle on the arm of her father, who gave her a kiss as she took her place at the front of church. Charles then sat down in the front row, putting his arm around Jenna as he leaned back in his chair.

Jeanne Martin, the well-known folk singer and songwriter, had grown up living next door to the Beckers and had taken keyboard lessons from Luna's Poppy. Jeanne always dropped by to say hello to them when she visited her parents. She had been quite taken with the story of a Moon girl marrying an Earth boy and moving to Mars. "It's so romantic," she had told May Becker. "It's so American, like moving to another continent and then crossing it in a covered wagon, just to be with the man you love."

May's response had been a bit tart. "I agree that indeed it's romantic and adventurous, but just remember I have only one grandchild, and in another year she will be gone forever. I'll never see her in person again and I'll never be able to hold my great-grandchildren at all."

Suddenly Jeanne had felt tears welling in her eyes. "I'd like to write a song for them, and later I'll write one for you and Professor Philip, and for Charles and Jenna too, in honor of the sacrifice all of you are making."

May's response had been to hug the younger woman, asking, "If you write a song for Luna and Michael, will you sing it at their wedding?"

That is why Jeanne Martin's first public performance of her greatest hit, "Love Fills The Universe," took place at Luna and Michael's wedding, leaving its listeners spellbound as the music of her clear soprano voice and twelve string guitar resonated in every crystal of the giant dome.

On this rare clear day, the Sun shone straight down upon the noontime ceremony, its bright rays scattered by the prisms of the dome's crystal crown into a rainbow of dancing lights that showered like confetti upon the wedding party. The glowing white satin dresses of the bride and her attendants shimmered with every hue in the spectrum as Luna and Michael spoke their vows beneath the perfect Crystal Dome they had helped to build.

the end